TEXANERS

I0681849

Étoile

Solitaire
Press

BY T. F. RHODEN

Fiction
Texaners: Eight Short Stories
published by étoile solitaire press
The Village
published by digital lycanthrope press

Non-Fiction
Burmese Refugees: Letters from the Thai-Burma Border
published by digital lycanthrope press

Travel
Yangon and Shwedagon Pagoda
published by other places travel guide
Chiang Mai and Northern Thailand
published by other places travel guide

Language
Karen Language Phrasebook: Basics of Sgaw Dialect
published by white lotus press
Making Out in Burmese
published by tuttle publishing
Outrageous Thai: Slang, Curses and Epithets
published by tuttle publishing

Texaners

eight short stories

T. F. Rhoden

Étoile Solitaire Press
Dallas

Étoile

Solitaire
Press

© T. F. Rhoden, 2015. Étoile Solitaire Press, Dallas, TX, USA.

Published by Étoile Solitaire Press, a division of 數字狼人.
ISBN-13: 978-0-692-51274-6
ISBN: 0-692-51274-8
City of Dallas, Republic of Texas, 75080, United States of America.

All rights reserved.

No part of this publication may be reprinted or reproduced, stored in a retrieval system, or transmitted in any form, by any means mechanical, electronic, photocopying, recording, or otherwise without prior permission from the author.

Earlier versions of some of these stories have appeared in literary magazines. "Oils" appeared in *The Monarch Review* and *Status Hat*. "The Gulf" appeared in *Foliate Oak Literary Journal*. "Drywall" appeared in *Microstory a Week*. "Airfare" appeared in *Weirdyear*. "Rooftop" appeared in *Black Heart Magazine*.

contact publisher via email
etoilesolitairepress@gmail.com

follow on twitter
@TFRhoden

visit author website
www.tfrhoden.com

TO KHIN SOE MON

Texaners

Contents

Remarks

I don't know that place people talk about when they talk about Texas.

Sometimes I think I've learnt more about the state the farther I've stumbled away from it. Not until I read Michener's *Texas* recently, at a safe distance on the other side of the globe, did the stereotype finally come together. I better understand that other conception of the place— *that* place—which acquaintances ever since my exodus have been indicating as being the real Texas.

Well, alas, now ya see, it ain't, quite, like that.

Or, at least, it never was for me and all those other million or so kids from the suburbs of Houston, Dallas, San Antonio, and Austin. Our middle-class demons of ennui were as tawdry and as precocious, and as loving, as any other set of children who were brought up in the relative safety and comfort of any of the innumerable suburbs across our super-sized nation.

This is all to say that we "Texans" are as boring as you are, assuming that you are American and that you bleed. This is also to say that we are as palpably multi-ethnic, multi-religious, multi-racial, multi-lingual, multi-cultural, multi-whatever as you are.

The title of this collection of short stories may appear to be a typo: Texan*ers*. There is some history to this particular epithet, homegrown in the Republic under six sordid flags as it were, but that is not why I chose it. We must pronounce it the way a German would. Emphasize the second syllable, like this: tex-AHHNN-ners. Make it sound foreign. It must be foreign if this book is to mean anything.

These stories are about new Texans—new *Texaners*. These children of the new Texas have no idea, no connection aside from locale, of that Texas of yesteryear. Some of these new Texaners might take pride in the whole fuck-you-we're-from-Texas thing, but I'm willing to bet it's more of a hipster-like affectation than anything really genuine. The majority of us simply don't care.

The invitation here is one of attempting a view of Texas and the Texaners which falls foul of a generality which is, I admit, probably more understandable, or at least more likeable for some, which of course really means more marketable. I wish to poo-poo the normal stereotypes.

We shall brook no cowboys or shit-kickers or ten-gallon hat thingies or horses or steers-or-queers references. This is not because they do not exist in Texas. They do somewhere I think. It is instead because I have no real knowledge, as a Texaner and as a writer, of any of that. My Texas youth involved 8-bit Nintendo NES, 7-Eleven Slurpees, and the occasionally poorly-administered handjob. That's it.

After nearly half a lifetime away, I can say with sincerity that I do not yearn so much for Texas or their Texans. I do, however, miss my Texaners. This collection is about them—those perfectly imperfect souls of expansive, yet common, diversity.

T. F. Rhoden, May 2015
Mae Sot, Thailand

Chinese Spoons

A sultry Kung-Pao-chicken smell inundated everything not made of steel. Its lukewarm stuffiness would waft, settle, and then burrow its way into clothing, chef hats, linen, order tickets, cash receipts, and the cardboard boxes of sunflower-seed oil stacked perilously high near the kitchen burners. The smell even seemed to find its way into the molding between the kitchen tiles, through to the concrete blocks holding up the Chang family restaurant in San Antonio, Texas.

Cindy poked her head past the Japanese *noren* curtain that separated the kitchen from the dining area. The waitress wondered where her order was.

—Diego! *Dónde está mi plato de Pat Thai y…*and another Kimchi?!

The two-foot dividing curtain was a double-sided rendition of Hokusai's famous color woodcut *Great Wave off Kanagawa*. Cindy's face was framed by the dark blues of undertow tides and crystal whites of crescent waves. Like a lone fisherman calling for help far out at sea, her voice was lost amongst the commotion of scatterbrained kitchen staff, busy with the chopping, dicing, and frying of Asiatic delicacies.

She called Diego's name again.

The Guatemalan heard her plea. His smile beamed in her direction:

—*Mi cuchara china?*

She could only guess at why the Guatemalan called her "Chinese spoon" in Spanish.

Like every teenage youth in Texas who was required to muddle through some Spanish courses to pass high school, Cindy knew enough of the language—even many of the spicier epithets taught to her by the schoolyard lotharios—to survive an afternoon in any North American kitchen. But she could not follow all of the head cook's odd phrasings.

Cindy repeated her order to Diego. It was interrupted by another voice.

—Fei! Is that you? Come back here quickly, a gravelly voice shouted in Cantonese.

—*Cuchara china,* your *padre* is calling you, said Diego, switching to English.

She moved to the back office beyond the kitchen. The other cooks, two from Mexico, another from Ecuador, looked up from their cutting boards and greasy woks as she passed.

Walking through the kitchen was like walking through a redolent fog: difficult to see where one was going, yet easy to sniff one's way past another order of fried eggrolls.

Another, more prismatic, curtain divided the kitchen from the closet-sized office.

—Fei! Look here, commanded Cindy's father, again using her Cantonese name.

He held up a plastic-coated menu.

—Check the English for your dear old pea of a father, Mr. Chang said and then chuckled.

Cindy received the menu and angled it under the office's florescent lighting so that the sheen struck away from her face.

The old pea's English was fine, Cindy thought. It had been over fifteen years now that their commercialized island of Hong Kong had been returned to the Middle Kingdom—over fifteen years that her father, mother, elder siblings and she had carpet-bagged their few-though-rich, belongings across the ocean on a Cathay Pacific flight to Los Angeles, and then from Los Angeles to San Antonio. Because she had been the one child of their family to commence her schooling completely on the North American continent, from elementary onwards, everyone in the household deferred to her as the authoritative expert on English.

Cindy fidgeted with the corner of the laminated card as she read:

—Pho, California Rolls, Chicken Satay, Kimchi, Pat Thai, Eggrolls, Edamame, Schezwan Pork, Tom Yam Gung, Kimbap…

What a ridiculous menagerie of Asian dishes, she wanted to retort.

Their family business had struggled ever since its inception. Had it not been for their Cantonese restaurant's prime real-estate within sight of the Alamo, the venture would have failed long ago. Tourists, so it seemed, often partook of Southern Chinese cuisine after ambulating about the Alamo—at least enough to have preserved the Chang family. But after a visit to a brother's eatery in the Twin Cities, Cindy's father had witnessed the success firsthand of going Pan-Asian. The rewards for embracing stereotypes appeared boundless. Mr. Chang had returned and remodeled everything to take advantage of the American penchant for benign diversity mingled with one-stop cultural immersion.

Cindy proffered a lame encomium and returned to the floor.

Diego halted her as she wended through the kitchen:

—*Pat Thai y Kimchi, Mi cuchara china*, said Deigo.

He nodded toward the order sitting atop the counter, cooling.

Before retrieving the order, Cindy stopped in front of the bilingual calendar posted next to the *noren* curtain. Though she knew that the date would not have changed since she last looked at it when she started this evening's shift, she hoped that the day would have somehow skipped forward, not just a few days, but a few months. They were still in October; she had six months until she would graduate from high school. Like her older siblings, she planned to do her tertiary studies as far away from the Chang family restaurant as possible. Though the day was not yet finished, she drew an X over the box with the current day's date.

*   *   *

Cindy poked the back of her classmate with her pen.

The boy, also a high school senior, lifted his head off his desk to see who had rustled him from his sleep. Seeing Cindy from the corner of his peripheries, he craned his neck up and looked toward the front of the classroom, wondering if the instructor had observed his slumbering.

The mathematics teacher was engrossed in an explanation of the Taylor polynomial in differential calculus.

Navarro, with a talent for analytic functions, was more interested in napping at the moment than relearning what he already understood. As long as he passed the advanced placement class with a low A-average, he was sure to garner college credit even before applying to some of the best universities in the nation for mathematics.

Ignoring both the girl behind him and the instructor

in front of the classroom, Navarro buried his head in his arms.

Cindy, undeterred, thrust her pen into Navarro's back again.

—What!?

Cindy laughed.

—Hey, what does *cuchara china* mean?

Navarro swiveled his behind in his chair to face the annoying Asian girl. He pondered both her question and the blackness of her tresses—how they framed her countenance prettily—before responding:

—It means "Chinese spoon."

—Yeah, I know that. I mean what does it mean in slang? Is it something bad?

Navarro said the word *cuchara* to himself. He looked quizzically at the girl.

—It doesn't mean anything. *Cuchara* just means spoon.

—Yeah, but is it some type of Mexican slang or something?

—No, not Mexican.

Cindy scrunched the side of mouth.

Navarro thought she resembled a Japanese anime character.

—Why? Who said *cuchara china* to you?

—Oh, it's nothing. Just the Guatemalan guy at work always calls me that.

—Guatemalan?

Navarro scoffed:

—Whatever. Guatemalans talk like retards. So I wouldn't know that slang. Ask Carlos. His parents are from there. Here, I'll get him for you.

Picking up a chewed-on easer, Navarro looked up to make sure the instructor was facing the other way before hurling the rubber across the room to hit Carlos on the shoulder.

The missile startled Carlos. The seventeen-year-old jumped in his seat.

—Hey, *puto*! What does *cuchara* mean? whispered Navarro.

Carlos, the class's sycophant, glared at Navarro. He mouthed the words:

—Stop bothering me.

—Huh? *Cuchara* means "stop bothering me"?

Navarro turned to Cindy:

—See what I mean. Guatemalans talk retarded Spanish.

Carlos overheard Navarro:

—You're the retard, you stupid Mexican wetback! Carlos shouted back in a whisper.

Navarro laughed:

—Who's calling who a wetback?

—*Cuchara* doesn't mean "stop bothering me", Carlos said, ignoring Navarro.

—*Cuchara* means "pussy", kind of like "coochie", you idiot!

Carlos was too vocal with the last curse word.

The instructor lifted her marker off the whiteboard and turned to the affronting pupil:

—Carlos, to whom, pray tell, were you speaking?

Carlos's face reddened to a fine puce:

—Sorry, Mrs. Kraft. I…uh…sorry.

Amidst the students' snickering, Navarro leant over Cindy's desk. He smiled, saying:

—*Cuchara china…*

Cindy's face also blushed rubicund.

Turning around to his own desk, Navarro spotted the notes Cindy had been taking:

—No, you copied it wrong. For higher-degree coefficients, they're determined by higher derivatives of f. So c needs to be $f'(x0)/2$, and d needs to be written like this $f''(x0)/3$ and so on. Otherwise you're going to mess it up and your line is going to look stupid.

Navarro removed the pen from Cindy's hand and corrected her notations.

He then dropped it on her spiral-bound notepad before turning back to his desk, hiding his head in his arms, and falling asleep.

* * *

Kathy nudged Cindy, foisting her attention to the family waiting to be seated at Mr. Chang's restaurant.

Cindy peered up from behind the bar area. Finished mixing the two overpriced mai-tais, she placed the cocktails on a black rubbery tray for Kathy.

—I think that's our congressman. Yeah, I can tell. I can remember his face from TV. That's him for sure, Kathy said, retrieving the concocted liquors.

—How is it you white people can always tell? Tep quipped.

Tep slid her way past Cindy and Kathy to retrieve some bottled beers. She uncapped three Asahis quickly, like tapping a pencil thrice in succession, and placed them on a tray.

—Because, oh, I don't know. Maybe because I'm educated and not a lazy Khmer princess like you, Kathy returned.

—Whatever. Cindy, let me have that table, then. All I've had tonight are black-tops and one cheap Mexican couple. I deserve at least one white-top, nah?

Cindy, in her semi-managerial role borne from being the daughter of the owner, acquiesced.

The Cambodian-American teenager smiled at Kathy as she slithered her way out of the bar area.

Tep's gait, as she walked to deposit the lager beers at her table, overemphasized a rolling motion in and out of her rump. Her hips were a velvety swing, like something a hip-hop singer might affect.

The three bachelors at her table stared at Tep as she walked toward them.

—Jeez, look at her. She thinks she's such a diva or something, Kathy murmured.

Cindy snickered. She went to receive the congressman and his family.

The congressman was threaded in casual, though expensive-looking, garb. His wife, too, looked rich, while their college-aged son appeared in ratty tee-shirt, unwashed shorts, and flip-flops. The son's hair was longish and his face feminine.

After sitting, the congressman seemed eager that his son talk to Cindy. He nudged his son.

Because the boy said nothing, holding his gaze away from Cindy, she told them that their waitress, Tep, would be with them shortly. Cindy returned to manage the bar.

Tep ambled to the congressman's table, offering another view of her rolling behind to her last table.

After a quick exchange of pleasantries, Tep looked dispirited, but then her face brightened again.

Tep waved for Cindy to come back to the congressman's table.

—I can't speak Chinese because I'm Cambodian. But Cindy can. Her family's from Hong Kong! Tep said, placing her hand on Cindy's shoulder as she walked up.

—Excellent! The congressman expounded. He then attempted to say hello in Chinese.

—Uhhh...*ni hao*, Cindy responded.

The congressman laughed. He pointed toward his wiry son across the table, and with raised eyebrows, exclaimed:

—That was a pretty good "new how," wasn't it? Our James here just spent the last summer learning Chinese in Peking, so he's been teaching me to say some things. He—

—Dad, it's *Beijing*, the boy interrupted his father. Only neo-liberal, neo-imperial orientalists call it "Peking".

The son grimaced. He then added:

—Nobody calls it "Peking" anymore. It's *Beijing*.

The congressman laughed:

—See, I'm learning new things all the time. Okay, so...James, order us dinner.

—But please don't order anything spicy, the congressman's wife chimed in.

—Oh, and son, see if you can't get me something with bread. Never been much of a fan of rice.

The son's face paled.

—Dad! yelped James. This is an *Asian* restaurant. They won't have bread. You have to get noodles or something.

—It's okay. We have bread, Tep interjected.

Tep smiled at the congressman.

Taking a solemn breath before beginning, like an amateur swimmer about to use the ten-meter platform for the first time, the congressman's son rattled off an incoherent stream of Chinese, pointing at the menu.

Cindy tried to smile:

—Oh, sorry. I don't really speak Mandarin. My parents are from Southern China, so we kind of like use Cantonese.

The congressman appeared confused. He did not understand Cindy's answer, as if Cindy had replied in some linguistically turgid tongue as opposed to her all-American, middle-class English.

The congressman's brows crinkled and his countenance dropped its false friendliness. He eyed his son, appealing for answers, but James only slinked farther back in his chair, like a remonstrated pet.

—See, dad, the congressman's son whined:

—I told you it would be stupid to try and order in Chinese. I mean, this isn't even a real Chinese restaurant. Look, they even serve Japanese food here...and Korean... and Thai and Vietnamese and I think that's Malaysian.

Tep kicked Cindy's shin.

—But, uhhh, try again, Cindy sputtered forth:

—Just, like, say it slowly because my Mandarin's not that good.

Cindy smiled as encouragingly as she could.

Tep smiled through an icy annoyance. She did not want Cindy mucking around with her tip.

The congressman's son, again, fumbled about in his awful Mandarin Chinese.

Cindy waited until the boy pointed at each item before writing it down, then handed the ticket to Tep.

—Sir, would you like garlic butter or just normal butter on your bread? Tep asked.

The congressman was pleased by the question. He gave the impression that his forthcoming answer would be the most important deliberation of his career.

—Why, yes, the man answered, confident:

—I believe I would like some...how do you say "garlic" in Chinese, son?

—*Da suan.*

—Yes, I would like a lot of "darn swans" in my butter.

Another couple bustled through the front door.

Cindy left Tep to her much-prized table of Caucasians.

Cindy went to greet and sit the new customers. She noticed that Navarro, from her calculus class, was one of the guests.

As they exchanged quick glances of recognition, Cindy saw an older, thin woman tarrying about behind Navarro. The old woman wore a grey-padded jacket over a hospital gown and loosely-fitting hospital trousers made of a cottony print of some popular cartoon characters. Her feet were nested in flimsy slippers.

—Oh, didn't know that this was your Asian restaurant? Navarro said by way of introduction.

His gaze fell upon the new décor. He was unsure if he was in the correct eatery:

—Do you guys still serve Chinese food here?

—Yeah, we do, Cindy said, retrieving two menus from the front stand:

—But we also have stuff from Japan and Korea and everywhere in Asia now.

Cindy indicated that Navarro and his companion should follow her.

Navarro took the elderly lady by the hand.

—She's my grandma. She's dressed like that because she's kind of crazy, Navarro explained to Cindy as they walked to his table.

Navarro made no attempt to lower his voice:

—Don't worry. She can't speak English. I'm just taking her out of the old folk's home for dinner. I tried to get the nurse to put some normal clothes on her, but she refused.

Navarro muttered something in Spanish and his grandmother sat down next to him.

Though the old woman's face was listless, the grandmother's body sat erect in perfect posture while her hands rested daintily in her lap. Some form of old-fashioned aristocratic breeding ran through her veins. Her heredity shone through her current comatose condition of geriatric prescriptions and was thrown into greater relief by her depressing garb.

Navarro, however, retained none of his grandmother's traits, physically or by way of personality. The matriarch was many shades lighter than her grandson, her skin color Anglo next to his. Navarro also displayed an impatience with everything around him, while his grandmother had a stoic understanding of her place in the cosmos. At first glance, they did not appear to be relatives. Most people would have assumed that Navarro was another young, Spanish-speaking male nurse taking a white, baby-boomer retiree out for a late afternoon stroll.

—Where are the eggrolls? Navarro questioned as he flipped over the new menu.

—Here. We also have springrolls. They're pretty good.

—Okay, I want ten eggrolls, Navarro commanded and flipped the plastic menu onto the table.

Cindy pulled out her ticket pad from her waitress's mini-apron and recorded the order. She waited for Navarro to continue, but he said nothing.

—And for you entrée? Cindy prodded him.

—No, that's it. Just eggrolls.

Cindy looked over at the elderly grandmother, who was staring straight ahead at some distant point that did not exist.

—Well, anything to drink? Cindy asked Navarro.

—Uhhh…for her, how about some water. And for me…I want a beer.

Cindy laughed, considering her classmate's proposal. She imagined how her father might react if he learnt that his daughter was selling alcohol to her underage class-mates.

—A beer? I don't know about that. If I bring you a beer, what are you going to do for me?

—I'll help you pass calculus, Navarro answered.

Cindy did not respond immediately. She pondered over the proposal.

—You mean like tutor me or something?

—Yeah, whatever works. We can meet after school, in the library or wherever. Maybe once a week.

Navarro smiled for the first time since entering the restaurant.

Unsure, Cindy responded:

—Okay, twice a week. But! Don't think you can come in everyday asking for beer, because I'm not going to give it to you.

Navarro's grin brightened as Cindy spun away from their table.

The three waitresses regrouped behind the bar: Kathy printed out a receipt from the restaurant's cash register; Tep fulfilled her drink order for the congressman's table; Cindy chose a beer at random for Navarro.

—The kid over there, Tep said to Kathey:

—He's more of an egg than you are.

Kathy looked over at the congressman's table:

—An egg?

—Yeah, he was trying to order his food in Chinese to Cindy. Kind of like how you're always trying to speak Chinese to Mr. Chang and he never understands you.

—Oh, whatever, shut up. My Mandarin's getting bet-ter. Plus I need to practice before I do my year abroad at Tsinghua University next year, Kathy defended herself.

Kathy added:

—What does that have to do with eggs?

—You know, white on the outside, yellow on the inside.

Tep laughed.

—That's stupid.

—It must be true, because I can see you're getting angry now.

—Ughhh, fine, if I'm an egg that makes you a...

Kathy's eyes peered over Tep's almond-brown face. She tried to think of something that was outwardly brownish, yet darker within:

—That makes you a meat pie!

—Meat pie, what the heck's that?

—It's that thing moms sometimes make: brown on the outside, black on the inside.

Cindy laughed this time.

Kathy pirouetted, shuffling away before Tep could retort.

—You know, I don't really like her, Tep confided to Cindy:

—I mean, if you're white, why would you even want to work at an Asian restaurant? It messes up the atmosphere and stuff.

—Like she said, she wants to practice Chinese before she leaves for her study abroad thing. Where else can a white girl get a chance to hear some Chinese in San Antonio than in a Chinese restaurant?

—Yeah, I guess so, Tep consented:

—Though in this restaurant? She's going to hear more Mexican than anything.

—Spanish, not Mexican.

—Whatever, but it still seems weird to me.

—You're just angry because she makes better tips than you do.

Annoyance flashed over Tep's face:

—Speaking of which, try not to mess up my tips, nah? Next time some white senator's son wants to talk you up in Chinese just go with it.

—Congressman's son, not senator's. You're lucky I even helped.

Tep finished filling up her three extra-large iced teas and moved to set the drinks on a cocktail tray. Smiling, she leant into Cindy before leaving:

—You know, the congressman's kind of good looking…in like that old-guy-with-power kind of way.

—What?!

Cindy followed Tep's gaze to the man in question:

—That's disgusting. He's all old and like fifty and married and…yuck!

—How much you want to bet if I ask for his number he gives it to me.

—Ugghhh, get out of here.

Tep obeyed Cindy's order and flittered away toward the congressman's table.

Cindy watched her friend quietly. The peculiar fragrance of reheated miso soup wafted from behind the curtain leading to the kitchen, reminding Cindy of the work at hand.

*　*　*

The school library was empty but for an overweight librarian and a group of three schoolboys huddled around one of the public computers. The homely librarian occasionally pestered the boys for being too loud but mainly she sat on her padded stool, mobile phone in hand. The air conditioners groaned painfully above, fighting against a very hot San Antonio sun in October. A baby green anole lizard had found its way into the library and now lay exhausted between two works by Philip Roth: neither had been checked out for forty-nine years.

The librarian eyed Cindy when she entered.

Cindy followed the lady's gaze to the circular wall clock hung above the group of boys.

—Is the library still open?

The librarian appeared irritated by the girl's interruption. Her fingers pecked at the plastic buttons on her mobile. She continued to type, ignoring Cindy's question. She shouted to the boys to lower their voices before lifting her gaze to Cindy.

—Did you miss your ride? Sorry, but you can't use the library phone to make calls. Call your parents from the payphone outside.

Cindy surveyed the library. Spotting a quiet-looking nook by two rows of shelves and out of view of the librarian, Cindy moved past the large woman's desk.

—Fine. You can wait here for your parents to pick you up, but I have to close up in an hour, the librarian relented as Cindy passed her:

—And don't put any books in your bag. The detectors are broken, okay?

Cindy deposited her backpack on the wooden table that was most hidden from anyone else's sight. She felt tired after a day's worth of high school frivolities. Removing one of the table's matching chairs, she sat down to wait for her new tutor.

Already she regretted arranging the meeting with Navarro, though she was not sure why. He was late, but that did not seem important. Something else nagged at her; something about the boy was beyond her ken. Even more than any of the other eighteen-year-old males knocking about the halls of their secondary school, Navarro seemed weirdly unfettered. The boy radiated emotion. Not effeminate emotion, Cindy ruminated, but a very angular-like emotion, like passion funneled through reason, or maybe feeling sifted through braininess. Navarro was bright, but odd.

The threesome of boys hanging on to each other in front of the library computer drew Cindy's attention. They appeared younger, probably in junior high. Cindy wondered why they had been allowed to enter the senior high school's library. She could see only a corner of the flat-panel screen that was glowing in their faces but surmised at what the boys were ogling. She marveled at their ability to hack past school-censured domains to reach their goal of pixilated pornography.

Navarro burst through the library's two doors. Seeing Cindy, he marched over to his classmate, disregarding the librarian's inquiries. He tossed his raggedy rucksack next to Cindy's.

—You're kind of late. We said we'd meet at three.

Navarro ignored the girl and fixed his attention on the group of freshman boys:

—What are those junior-high kids doing here? This library's for senior high only.

Not waiting for Cindy's response, Navarro strolled up to his younger classmates. The freshmen peered up from their digital profligacy to see him hovering over them.

—Mrs. Gutiérrez! These junior high idiots are looking at porn! Navarro railed across the room.

At the sound of unrestrained commotion, the librarian's fat head popped up like a pig shot from a circus cannon. Mrs. Gutiérrez plopped down from her perch sprightlier than her bodily girth would have suggested possible. Arming herself with a yard ruler, she charged at the offending youths. Multifarious Spanish epithets involving a virgin named Mary ignited from her mouth as she chased the boys out of her library. A good, sheep-like Catholic most of the time, Mrs. Gutiérrez, in times of duress, knew how to marshal the inner shepherd. Combating the iniquity of erotic art was a most noble crusade. She beat the boys away from her domain.

The librarian thanked Navarro before returning to her stool.

—I hate freaking freshmen, Navarro said to Cindy, taking a seat next to hers.

Navarro extended his legs, leant back in his chair, folded his hands together, and stared at Cindy before inquiring:

—So, what do you want to know?

Cindy rummaged through her multicolor bag and pulled out her advanced-placement mathematics text-book and some other crinkled papers with many multi-tiered formulas freckling their surfaces. She handed one of the least creased sheets to her classmate.

—Most of these functions are kind of easy, you know? Navarro commented after pondering the paper's contents for a moment.

—Why did you take AP calculus? Navarro questioned, placing the sheet onto the table.

—I'm okay at math and so I wanted to get some more college credit before I leave here. I already did college algebra, so figured I'd do the college calculus one too, Cindy answered.

—But you have to get an A. Otherwise, most colleges won't give you credit for it. Did you get an A in college algebra? But then again any retard can get an A in college algebra, right?

Navarro laughed:

—But AP calculus class is more difficult, not for me or anything, but I think for most of people because it starts to go into differential equations, mean values, implicate functions and whatever. If you don't pull an A, then you'll be kind of wasting your time.

Cindy sighed:

—Yeah, I know I have to get an A, okay? So, can you help or not?

The boy smiled:

—Well, yeah, I said I would.

Navarro retrieved the worksheet from the table and scanned over the contents once more. He then set the paper back down.

—I'm surprised you're going to let me help you though. I wouldn't have thought one of the popular girls would want to been seen with me.

Cindy blinked at her classmate.

Why such an offbeat question was ushered, Cindy could not fathom. She was uncertain how to respond to such a ridiculous statement:

—What? What are you talking about? What does this have to do with helping me understand calculus? …and popular what? I'm not popular.

—Yeah, you are.

—Uhhh, no! The only popular girls in this school are Mexican. How could I possibly be popular?? Asian Americans are never popular, especially in San Antonio.

Cindy's last confession gave Navarro pause.

—Well, maybe you're not popular, but you're exclusive, Navarro replied, searching for the correct word.

—Huh? Now who's being retarded?

—No, you kind of are. You and Tep and Kathy, you've got like your own little group, kind of like an Asian club or something going on.

—I work with Tep and Kathy everyday! And they're my friends. That's why I'm always with them!

If Cindy had known that Navarro would be such a bother, she never would have traded a beer for tutoring sessions.

—What, then? You want to join our "Asian club" or something? Cindy returned.

—Well, maybe. Maybe I do want to hang out with you some time. I've started Japanese class this semester. So I also want to learn more about Asian culture and stuff, Navarro admitted.

Navarro's face was stoically preemptive for rejection.

—I'm Chinese!! Cindy exploded.

—Well, it's kind of the same thing, except of course for that spat you had during World War II.

—What!? You mean like where the Japanese came and attacked us and put in a puppet regime and how the Rape of Nanking happened!? There's a big difference there. How would you like it if I called you a Guatemalan?

—I guess I'd get annoyed.

—Yeah, exactly, so don't call me Japanese!

—But I didn't call you Japanese. I just said that I'm taking—

—Whatever! Can we do this math already? Cindy interrupted.

Cindy's mobile phone rang. She rushed to answer the melodic contraption before the librarian had time to descend from her perch. After a quick conversation of fewer than three mutterings, she ended the call. Cindy looked at the mobile's timepiece.

—I have to go, she murmured.

Retrieving the worksheet that lay in front of Navarro, Cindy gathered together her other books, shoving everything into her backpack.

—Already? But we haven't done anything yet?

—Yeah, I know. But you were late and then you insisted on talking about I don't know what. I have to go to work.

Tep and Kathy entered the library.

Seeing their friend in the corner, they walked toward her, ignoring the librarian and her shopworn pleas for quiet. They halted in front of the tête-à-tête.

Tep grinned out of the corner of her mouth.

—Since when are you into the Latin thing? I thought you liked white guys.

Tep laughed through her teeth.

—Shut up, Tep.

Cindy tossed on her backpack to leave. She joined her friends.

—When do you want to meet again? Navarro asked.

The three girls turned to look upon the Mestizo boy.

As a group, standing together in a line, Navarro imagined the trio to be a three-headed hydra capable of spitting venom: Cindy peering down at Navarro, Tep with her hand on her bare-skinned hip, Kathy eyeing the boy as if he were some inexhaustible nuisance. He wished he had not asked.

—Maybe I don't really need a tutor, but thanks anyway.

Knowing he would not respond, Cindy twirled around to exit.

Her two comrades followed approvingly.

*　*　*

Mr. Chang pulled his shirt out from his trousers and

loosened his belt a notch. In anticipation of his meal, the proprietor was already preparing himself for the eventual growth in girth. When his restaurant All Asian Delights had still been named Mr. Chang's Cantonese Cuisine, the cornucopia of dim sum dishes for sale had seemed infinite: Pork Char Siu Baau, Shrimp Gao, Duck Egg Congee, No Mai Gai, Chicken Phoenix Claws, Taro Dumplings, Crab Roe Shaomai… In the changeover to profitability though, Mr. Chang had insisted on keeping only one of these delicacies: broiled chicken feet.

Mr. Chang stood up from his office chair to retrieve his favorite spirit from the prefab shelving above his desk.

When Mr. Chang was still in his twenties, he had been a busboy at an upscale bar facing Hong Kong's Kowloon Park, frequented by lonely bachelors in the British civil service. One rakish Scotsman had taken a liking to the younger Chang and would always sneak shots of his Islay whisky to the impressionable young man whenever Chang happened past his solitary table. Ever since then—whenever Mr. Chang had had the funds for such things—he insisted on drinking only Laphroaig ten-year-old single malt, cask strength whisky. He had discovered very early that the liquor's husky peat somehow balanced the tanginess of a chicken's broiled foot perfectly. Any other spirits, including the traditional Chinese rice wines and über-popular Johnny Walker-branded whiskies, paled in comparison to the strangely tasty coupling that Laphroaig and Cantonese-sauced chicken feet promised.

Pouring himself a healthy portion of whisky into an unwashed coffee cup, Mr. Chang saw Tep enter the office with his plate of chicken feet and bowl of steamed rice.

Tep placed the viands in the middle of his desk, ignoring the opened accounting books and stray sheets of receipts and invoices that covered every surface.

As she leaned over to unsheath a pair of throwaway chopsticks and place them on the side of the plate, Mr. Chang caught a glimpse down the front of her shirt. Her bra was padded, he noticed. But the sight was tantalizing.

Mr. Chang munched on his chicken feet, ignoring the rice. He drank his Laphroaig.

Having finished his meal and feeling aglow from the single malt, Mr. Chang left his office for the restaurant floor. He stopped in the kitchen for a few moments to look over the shoulders of his kitchen staff. Mr. Chang made as if they were preparing something incorrectly, suggested that the cook Diego add more of this, less of that, and ordered one of the younger ones to mop the floor.

Everyone knew this was more a show of Mr. Chang brandishing himself as if he were still in control. Diego and his crew played along with their boss's superfluity. They pretended to listen and obey, when in truth they knew how to cook most of the dishes on the menu better than the owner.

Mr. Chang moved onto the restaurant floor and surveyed the early evening crowd.

Business seemed light. Only a few tables had customers. However, his waitstaff, his three girls, Cindy, Kathy, and Tep, appeared busy, so he found himself feeling pleased.

Kathy came up to the soda fountain to refill a drink. She paused to say something to Mr. Chang in Mandarin, to which he responded in his slippery Cantonese.

Mr. Chang liked that this San Antonio girl was learning Chinese, but he refused to use what he saw as "mainlander's language", the government-proscribed Mandarin, even though his own communist Putonghua was just fine.

A customer appeared at the front. With his waitresses engaged in their own tables, Mr. Chang decided to seat the new patron himself.

Mr. Chang's welcome was cut short by the customer's question:

—Hi. Is Cindy here?

Mr. Chang surmised that the youth in front of him was not a paying customer.

—She's busy, Mr. Chang replied.

—Yeah, I know, but I'm…I'm like her tutor and I need to arrange something with her real quick, the youth responded.

Mr. Chang eyed him before calling his daughter over.

Cindy looked up from where she was bussing a table. She was not sure why, but Cindy felt her face redden when she saw Navarro lurking near the menu lectern.

Mr. Chang realized that this high-school boy was a friend, so he let the two of them be, but not before warning his daughter in Cantonese not to dawdle.

Cindy glared at Navarro. She asked him what he wanted.

—Nothing. I was just going to ask why you didn't show up for me to tutor you today?

Cindy wondered why the answer to that was not obvious. Had she not already made herself clear after their last lesson last week? But because Navarro sounded despondent when he asked, she doubted whether she was in the right or not.

Cindy stammered, feeling exasperated:

—All we did was argue last time. You didn't even teach me anything.

Navarro's face broke into a smile and then he laughed:

—Yeah, I guess you're kind of right. But it's okay. I promise to be a better tutor this time.

Cindy wanted to say no, but instead sputtered:

—Fine.

Navarro placed his hand over his heart, still smiling:

—And next time, I promise we'll actually go over some stuff that's important.

—All right, fine, Cindy responded again.

She saw her father watching them from across the restaurant floor:

—Hey, I'm busy. Can we talk about this later?

—All right, awesome, but was going to say I think we should study in the public library as well. The school one is loud and closes too early. And I can give you a ride to work afterwards, too.

Another group of customers came in behind Navarro.

—I'll let you take care of them, Navarro said, smiling once more before leaving.

Cindy wondered to what she had consented.

* * *

Cindy's elementary, middle, and high schools had been built next to each another, along a single street in one of the northern suburbs of San Antonio.

The buildings, like the children inside them, seemed to get progressively taller as one passed through the educational system. Between each of the schools had been planted crapemyrtle trees, forever resistant to the southern Texas heat. A group of ten- and eleven-year-old boys were chasing each other between the elementary and middle schools. One boy grabbed and tore from one of the crapemyrtles a bushel of pinkish deciduous leaves. Delighted with himself, he launched his new missile at an unsuspecting friend running toward him. The bushy bundle exploded on contact, ricocheting pink leaves in a hundred directions. One of the adults, parked in her car, waiting for school to let out, chided the boys to cease destroying the landscape. The boys laughed and escaped from sight to the back of the school.

Cindy's attention was drawn away from the elementary students when she saw Navarro pull up in front of the high school.

Without leaving the driver's seat, Navarro leant across the passenger side to open the door of his three-decade-old Bronco as Cindy descended the high school's front steps. Though somewhat dirty with age, the car seemed as if it had been cleaned recently.

Inside, Cindy noticed that various knobs and handles seemed completely worn down or to be missing. When she asked Navarro where the seatbelt was, he snorted:

—Don't worry about that. This beast is made of steel. We're fine.

Cindy saw that Navarro wore his seatbelt though.

The distance from high school to their public library was not far, even within walking distance, but the weather was hot and both Navarro and Cindy had been raised at the peculiar income level where walking for utility—as opposed to sport—was shameful.

As they reached the library, Navarro did not slow down. When Navarro drove beyond the entrance to the library parking lot, Cindy became nervous:

—Uhh, you just drove past the library.

—I know. I have to drop something off real quick to my grandma. It won't be long.

Navarro pointed to some groceries in the backseat. He drove for another five minutes before slowing down in front of the one of the city's many assisted-living facilities. Parking the car, Navarro said:

—Don't worry. I'll be back in a sec. You can just wait

in the car.

Cindy looked at the bags of groceries in the backseat. She felt silly not helping, so when Navarro exited the vehicle, Cindy followed.

—Are you sure you want to come inside? It kind of smells in there.

—I'll just help you carry these. Then we can get to the library and study.

Navarro said nothing.

Inside the reception area of the complex, the atmosphere ranged from stale to fuggy.

The black receptionist, dressed in medical grab decorated with cartoon characters, had them sign in. She led them down one of the poorly lit hallways. All of the seniors they passed were dressed in various types of nightwear, some in pajamas shirts and trousers, others in single tees that stretched down to their unsightly ankles. Sometimes Navarro and Cindy had to press their backs against the walls to let the occasional wheelchaired geriatric pass. Odd shouts could be heard faintly down the other end of the building. The receptionist told them to ignore those: dementia was common, she warned them.

—Mrs. Patricio, *tiene invitados*! the receptionist sang after they had entered Navarro's grandmother's room without knocking.

The receptionist's Spanish was mustered with a Southern twang, but it was understandable.

Mrs. Patricio had the television set on with the volume at near maximum, but she was not paying any attention to it. She was seated with her back to the tube, looking out of her window onto the apartment complex's ill-kempt garden below.

The receptionist nurse flipped the overhead lights on and off a few times before reaching for the remote to mute the television.

—Mrs. Patricio, your son has come to visit you, the receptionist announced again, this time in English.

When Mrs. Patricio did not respond, the nurse shrugged and exited the room, leaving the youths to do as they pleased with the old lady.

Navarro and Cindy laid the few groceries on top of the two-person table in the corner. Aside from some fruit, the goods were dry foods or hygiene products.

Navarro went up to his grandmother and placed his hand on her shoulder. He spoke to her softly, but Mrs. Patricio did not respond.

Mrs. Patricio continued her benumbed surveillance of the garden area as if she were expecting some exigency to spring forth. Her eyes were fixated on a bush of violet mountain laurel that needed watering.

When Navarro spoke a second time, Mrs. Patricio awoke from her trance. She allowed him to help lift her from her chair and steer her around the room's scant furniture toward where Cindy was seated, unpacking the groceries.

—Mom wanted me to bring these to you. Look, I got some *granada* fruit from the Mexican grocers, your favorite, Navarro said to her in Spanish, sitting her across from Cindy.

Mrs. Patricio's eyes shone when she spotted the yellow-orange fruit. Cindy picked up one of the hard-shelled fruits.

—In Spanish, *granada* means "pomegranate", right? Cindy asked Navarro.

—Yeah, I think so, but this isn't a pomegranate. I think you call it "passion fruit" in English. It tastes a little more sour and better. Or maybe there are the same species? I'm not sure really. But in Spanish it's *granadilla*. Or if you're

Mexian we just call it *granada* or *granada de moco*.

Navarro paused and then laughed:

—Actually my grandma calls it *granada china* for some reason. From China, like you, I guess.

Cindy tried to peel off the shell:

—I think we need a knife.

—No, not really. Watch my grandma do it. She's been eating this stuff since she was a kid. She used to tell me that they grew them on their plantation in Veracruz like way back when.

Navarro handed a passion fruit to Mrs. Patricio. Without much effort the eighty-four-year-old woman managed to stick her thumbs into the shell in one place and crack the fruit open without spilling any of the viscous pulp within.

—This fruit is the only thing that seems to wake her up from her Alzheimer's haze. Otherwise, she doesn't really say much or do much or recognize what's going on around her, Navarro commented.

Cindy watched as Mrs. Patricio ate the fruit without a knife or spoon.

A man in an ill-fitting suit and tie appeared at the doorway. He introduced himself as the centre's managing director and asked if Navarro could discuss something about payments in the office. Navarro left Cindy with his grandmother, promising to be no more than a few minutes.

With Navarro gone, Cindy wondered if they might ever get to the library and begin studying. A midterm exam had been scheduled for the end of next week. She was nervous about it.

—Navarro is a smart boy, a good boy, Mrs. Patricio said suddenly in Spanish, interrupting Cindy's thoughts.

—Especially since he didn't have a father to raise him.

That stupid *campesino* father of his. I will never understand why my daughter got involved with someone so low. But it doesn't matter. He's not a problem anymore. He's probably drunk in some alleyway in Jalapa, nearly dead by now I should think.

Mrs. Patricio's sudden cogency startled Cindy.

Every word that came out of Mrs. Patricio's mouth carried a stately lilt. Despite the stuffy atmosphere of the room and geriatric-looking dress, something debonair radiated from her person. Mrs. Patricio seemed as if she had been misplaced somehow, tricked into living out her remaining years in a common world by uncommon hands.

From what Navarro said, Cindy had not expected his grandmother to be able to hold a conversation. Maybe the fruit had somehow sparked a few of Mrs. Patricio's neurons back to life. Cindy understood only about half of what Navarro's grandmother said.

Mrs. Patricio stared at the girl sitting across from her, inquiring:

—Are you my grandson's girlfriend?

—Uhhh...no, Señora Patricio. *Somos sólo amigos*, Cindy answered, happy that she could remember this line in Spanish.

—*Amigos*? the old woman returned.

A smile inched across Mrs. Patricio's countenance:

—*Amigos*...

Mrs. Patricio cracked open another passion fruit, handing half to Cindy.

—Here, *granada china* is good for the skin.

Navarro came back into the room to find his grandmother and Cindy munching on fruit:

—I guess we can go now. You want to study, right?

—Navarro! Mrs. Patricio cut off her grandson:

—Aren't you going to introduce me to this young lady?

Navarro was taken aback by his grandmother's question.

—Nana, you're awake? Navarro sputtered forth in Spanish.

—Of course your nana is awake, Mrs. Patricio snapped.

Navarro, tickled to see that his grandmother could still be her old self, introduced Cindy to her.

Mrs. Patricio berated her grandson for not visiting more often. She also invited Cindy to come back and visit her whenever she pleased.

They spent half an hour at the senior living centre before leaving.

Once inside the public library, after Navarro and Cindy had settled at a quiet table at the back of the building, Navarro commenced his lesson. Unlike the last time, Navarro and Cindy were able to find a working rhythm. Navarro concentrated on tutoring, Cindy on learning.

* * *

—Tep called in sick, so it's only you two girls tonight, Mr. Chang informed Cindy and Kathy in his office:

—It's only a Tuesday, so there won't be many customers. If it gets busy, I'll help out.

Mr. Chang sat in his faux leather chair facing Cindy and Kathy.

Both the girls, Cindy leaning against her father's desk, Kathy against the opposite unwashed wall, kept their hands pocketed in their waitress's aprons as Mr. Chang spoke.

Cindy complained that her father should hire another server. Kathy concurred, reminding her boss that she would be departing at the end of the school year. Cindy was going to mention the same thing—that she was going to leave as well—but decided it was better to hold her say: No reason to have that argument now, she thought.

Mr. Chang said that he agreed, but Cindy knew he would not bother to hire anyone new. If the restaurant needed additional work staff, then she would have to find them like she did Kathy and Tep.

Diego stuck his head through the curtain. Smiling, he leered at the teenage girls before speaking to Mr. Chang:

—Mr. Chang, no more cilantro, no more...*tomatera y ajo*.

—Have the Ecuadorian kid go to the store and stock up on whatever we need, Mr. Chang ordered, pulling two twenty-dollar bills from the cashbox:

—But make sure he gets a receipt.

Cindy translated for Diego in case he did not understand.

Diego's eyes brightened as Mr. Chang relayed the money to his head chef.

The girls followed Diego out of Mr. Chang's cluttered office.

The evening progressed as Mr. Chang foresaw; few patrons came, and those that did barely left any tips.

The girls began to prepare the restaurant for the end of the night early, wiping down tabletops, chairs, and menus, sweeping out corners, refilling soy sauce bottles, arranging cloth napkins, Chinese spoons, wooden chopsticks, and the occasional fork. The kitchen staff, too, began to clean everything that was not being currently used.

Fifteen minutes before closing, Navarro appeared at the front door.

Cindy, annoyed that a customer was coming so late, smiled when she saw that it was Navarro.

Cindy and Navarro had continued their weekly tutoring session for four weeks. She had done well on her midterm test and was looking forward to tomorrow when they would be reviewing material for their last meeting of the semester before their final week of examinations this fall.

—It's kind of late. The kitchen's already closed, Cindy greeted him.

—Really, the sign outside said you're still open? I just wanted to order some eggrolls to go.

—I'm just kidding. We're still open, Cindy replied.

She walked over to the faintly buzzing neon open-sign and switched it off:

—I'm too lazy to serve anyone after you, though. You just want some eggrolls? How many?

—Like five is fine.

Cindy invited Navarro to sit at the small bar area next to the cash register at the back of restaurant. Cindy placed the order and disappeared into the kitchen.

Diego cursed when Cindy gave him the order, complaining that he had already shut off the fryer.

She told him to turn it back on.

When she returned she saw Navarro's looking at the décor behind the bar: some prints with Japanese script, a Korean kerchief from the 2002 World Cup, some Buddhist wind catchers from Northern Thailand, a few framed landscapes of Hong Kong's harbor at dusk. The silhouette of a Chinese junk drifted peacefully in one picture.

Navarro asked her if people used those junks for cargo anymore or if they were only for tourists, like the docile boats that floated along San Antonio's river walk. She said that she could not remember.

Cindy's mobile rang. She saw Tep's name glowing from

the display screen.

When Tep started speaking Cindy understood immediately that something was wrong.

Tep's usual sangfroid was absent. Cindy knew her friend well enough to recognize that she had either just been crying or was shaken. She sounded fearful of something.

—Tep, what's wrong?

Tep did not answer.

—Where are you now? Why didn't you come in tonight?

Cindy felt suddenly frightened herself.

—Can you come pick me up? Tep finally spoke. Her voice sounded lifeless.

Cindy again asked where she was. Tep answered that she was at a motel, one of the nondescript ones beyond the super highway that cinctured downtown San Antonio.

—Are you okay?

—yeah, Tep murmured.

—Okay, but I don't have a car.

—Ask Kathy. Use her car. Just hurry if you can. I want to leave here.

Tep ended the call.

Cindy began to explain to Kathy that they needed to leave.

Kathy, initially incredulous, could not understand why Tep was at a motel and why she might need a ride away from one. But Kathy too began to feel an urgency after listening to Cindy's supplication.

Kathy apologized. She did not have her car with her; she had let her younger brother borrow it for the evening.

Now Kathy was anxious. She wanted to know too what had happened to Tep. She nodded toward Navarro, suggesting maybe Cindy's classmate might be of use.

Diego called out that the order of eggrolls was fin-ished. He asked if anymore diners were on the floor.

Ignoring him, Cindy retrieved the grease-stained bag of eggrolls, placing the to-go order in front of Navarro.

—Hey, do you think you can give me a ride real quick?

—And me, too, Kathy chimed in, moving next to Cin-dy behind the bar.

—Sure. You need a ride home?

—Well, not really. We just need to pick up a friend real quick. You know Tep, right? And then come back here. She's just over on 410, near the airport...I think, Cindy explained.

Navarro groaned when she mentioned the interstate loop, but he agreed.

Cindy yelled out to her father still in the back office in Cantonese:

—Dad! The restaurant's closed. I have to go some-where with Kathy real quick. I'll be back in like half an hour!

Diego came out from behind the sodden kitchen. Cindy saw him as they were leaving.

—That's it for today, Diego. *Vete a casa*! Cindy said as they slipped out the front.

Neither Diego nor Mr. Chang had time to respond.

Inside Navarro's Bronco, driving north toward the air-port, Navarro ignored the girls. He ate his eggrolls, one hand on the wheel, the other occasionally dipping the deep-fried treat into a portion cup of sweet and sour sauce he had placed in the divider cup holder.

After having punched in the motel address into her phone, Cindy told Navarro where to turn off the highway.

As they were pulling into the motel's parking lot, Cindy wondered whether she had navigated them to the correct place. She looked up at the sign and realized that they were at the motel that belonged to a longtime friend of Mr. Chang. One quick glance at the upside-down Chinese character placed atop some gold-lettered Vietnamese script on the motel's office door was enough to confirm that the establishment was owned by her father's friend.

Not seeing Tep anywhere on the premises, Cindy and Kathy left Navarro in his car to visit the room number Tep had given Cindy.

They hurried along the pathway, counting the brass numbers of each door they passed.

Many of the walkway's lights were missing, while the one's that did work shone with an ugly yellow strobe. Overhead they could hear a commercial jet ascending. The buildings shook with every liftoff.

They knocked at the room number Tep had indicated. A shadow descended over the peephole.

Tep pulled the door open. Behind her the lights were turned off, so that the girl appeared as if she were coming out from a cave.

As Tep leant down to pick up her multicolor purse from the nightstand, Kathy shoved her way past Cindy and Tep, barging into the room, flipping on the overhead light.

—No, don't! Tep whimpered.

Cindy and Kathy stared at the dirty room with its aged fixtures, greasy walls, soiled carpets, and old curtains. The bed was unmade, the off-white sheets and brown cotton blanket crumbled off to one corner of the mattress.

—I just want to go! Tep pleaded.

The room with its sallow lights and the genuine fear in Tep's eyes seemed otherworldly.

Cindy and Kathy realized what had taken place in the grimy motel room. But because everything seemed so awkwardly beyond the pale of their suburban lives, they stood dumbfounded, unable to move or say anything. Such unwashed, denuded licentiousness was a shock to them. Even though both Cindy and Kathy had necked with boys before, both felt vestal compared to this scene.

Cindy then saw the side of Tep's face: the skin over her left cheekbone was a darker umber than her normal color.

—Tep, your face!? Cindy yelped.

Blushing, the girl pivoted her bruised face away from her friends and moved toward the open door.

Both Cindy and Kathy stopped her.

Tep seemed to lose grip of the last remaining vestiges of whatever equanimity the seventeen-year-old was clinging on to. She let herself fall down in a chair and covered her face as tears began to swell in her brown eyes.

—What happened!? Kathy was indignant:

—Who were you with just now? Someone from school? You just can't get hit in the face and not do something about it. We should call the police.

—No, don't, Tep cried.

—Then tell us what happened! Kathy yelled.

Kathy already had her phone out to make a call.

Cindy placed her hand on Kathy's shoulder and shook her head.

—Who was with you? Cindy asked quietly, as a mother does to a small child who wishes to glean information from her kin.

Cindy pulled up the room's other wooden chair in front of her friend and sat.

Tep did not want to reveal whom she had just been with. But a glance at her friend's faces told her that she should:

—I was with the congressman.

Cindy exchange glances with Kathy.

—What? Kathy queried.

—The congressman, Tep repeated.

Tep wiped away some tears.

With her quick confession, the girl was already stifling her sudden ebullition. Though still emotional, Tep's sturdy fatalism was acting as an analgesic to the situation. What would have torn apart Cindy and Kathy's overprotective understanding of the world was instead succoring the realities that Tep, though still a teenager, had come to acknowledge as coeval with their species.

Cindy and Kathy stared at Tep, mystified.

Tep continued:

—The congressman, remember? He came into the restaurant like a month ago. He gave me his business card when his wife and kid were in the bathroom. And then I called him and I guess we've started messing around a bit. And so tonight he brought me here.

Cindy and Kathy did not know how to respond.

—We were joking about something just now and so I said he should buy me the new iPhone. And then just kidding, I added if he didn't I would tell everyone that he was with an underage girl. And then he like flipped out and got all scared and slapped me really hard and said I shouldn't talk like that. He was muttering something to himself and then yelled that we can't see each other anymore and that if I said anything I would get into trouble at school and that my parents would lose their refugee status. I told him I had only been kidding, but he didn't listen. Then he put on his pants and just left. I didn't have a ride home so I called you.

Though another wave of moral indignation was rising inside of Kathy as she listened to her friend's confession, Tep's matter-of-fact admission and resignation in listing her evening's exploits suppressed Kathy's otherwise righteous misgivings.

Cindy, too, felt off-kilter as she followed Tep's story.

Both Cindy and Kathy could not understand what could have attracted their friend to the satyr.

Two honks from Navarro's car outside ended the girls' conversation.

Cindy looked through the window blinds and saw Navarro waving.

When Tep rose to leave this time, her friends did not stop her.

Tep's embarrassment riled anew when she saw that they had not taken Kathy's car to retrieve her.

—Sorry to honk, but the owner came over here and said that I can't park here if I'm not going to get a room, Navarro apologized as the girls climbed into his Bronco.

All three sat in the back bench seat.

As they were leaving, Tep asked if she could spend the night at Cindy's house, indicating she did not want her parents to see her face.

Cindy worried that her own parents might have a similar reaction to Tep that she had had.

Though Kathy was still incensed, Tep's unwillingness to return home and see her parents was an admission for Kathy that Tep understood something of her own iniquity. Kathy purposed that they sleep over at her place since her parents were out of town. The other two concurred, instructing their driver to shuttle them to Kathy's.

Cindy noticed the motel proprietor staring at them as they left the motel parking lot. His unfriendly countenance worried her. When her own cell phone lit up with an incoming call from the restaurant, Cindy already knew that her father's friend must have identified her. Refusing to answer the call, she suggested that Navarro drop off Kathy and Tep first. She asked Navarro to drive her by Mr. Chang's restaurant once more.

Cindy sensed a coming tempest of angry questions and accusations of unfilialness from her father. She sighed.

Beams of fluorescence highlighted Cindy's anxious face every time the Bronco rhythmically passed under one of the speedway's lampposts.

The radiance of downtown San Antonio whirled about all the passengers, dicing the nighttime air into fine slivers of urban incandescence.

*   *   *

Navarro let the Bronco's husky-sounding engine run for ten minutes before turning off the contraption. Cindy had requested him to wait for her outside the restaurant. Before running inside, she had murmured that she would need two or three minutes to retrieve something.

Unsheathing his phone from his pocket, Navarro saw that the time had already crept past midnight. Even though tonight was a school night, he did not fret about rushing home. He could have returned at three in the morning and his mother would not have reprimanded him, Navarro ruminated. Since his mother's nursing shift started at nine in the evening, she would not be due back till sometime between five and six the next day. On evenings like tonight, when he ate away from home, their schedules meant that they would miss each other. Navarro realized that he spent more time with his grandmother than he did with his own mother these days.

Still seated in the driver's side, waiting, Navarro turned away from Mr. Chang's toward the empty strip mall.

From afar, on the opposite end of the football field-sized parking lot, Navarro noticed a garbage truck turn the corner and drive in his direction. The yawing pit of refuse in the back occasionally released a torn plastic bag or small sting of paper into the air as the truck came nearer. The two neon-vested workmen dangling onto the sides of the vehicle ignored the escaping debris. The truck halted in front of an industrial dumpster, initiating the unfurling of the vehicle's claws. Beneath the hissing sounds of pressurized hydraulics, the Spanish-speaking workmen jibed with each other. Their raucous joking was loud enough for Navarro to hear inside his car. As the mechanical beast began to lift the dumpster, a deep clang resounded from within, as if something had shifted inside the trash receptacle. The workmen shouted to the driver to stop and lower the grainy dumpster. Inside they found a metal car bumper, slightly dented, but obviously still of value from the cries of excitement of the workmen. Navarro guessed the bumper belonged to one of those oversized pickup trucks from the previous century, maybe a Chevy, maybe a Ford—the shiny piece of metal produced abroad—but the brand, the essence, certainly American.

The signage outside Mr. Chang's restaurant turned off, ceasing to glow.

Carrying her school pack, Cindy exited from the front doors and locked them before scurrying toward Navarro's Bronco. She flung her backpack into the back as she sat in the passenger's side.

Navarro realized that she had been crying:

—You want me to just drop you off at Kathy's?

Cindy nodded.

—Are you all right? Navarro asked as he pulled onto the speedway.

Cindy did not want to explain to him about the argument she had just had with her father. Mr. Chang's friend had phoned him as Cindy had foreseen. Cindy's father had wanted to know what Cindy, and his other two other waitresses, had been doing at his friend's execrable motel. Since she dared not tell him the true reason, the quarrel had somehow digressed into other more immediate familial topics.

Cindy had let slip that she wanted to quit the family business like her older siblings next year, which had only escalated the dispute.

Before she had walked out, her father had shouted something about not coming back.

Though Cindy knew he was not serious, the passion behind her father's command had struck her painfully.

When Cindy did not respond to Navarro, he asked another question:

—What was up with the crappy motel anyway? Why was Tep there?

Cindy was slow to respond:

—It was nothing.

Cindy could tell that Navarro felt incensed at her non-response.

Navarro stopped forwarding any more questions.

Cindy was reminded of Tep's problem. Though she could sympathize with her friend, Cindy still could not fathom how she could have involved herself in something like that. Cindy wondered if it might not be wiser to follow Kathy's suggestion; maybe they should tell the police or someone with authority.

She was reminded of those bromidic posters often placated outside of the high school counselor's office, the ones with pathetic imagines of unfashionably dressed teenagers looking sorry for themselves, always with a hotline to call or address to contact. But then again, Cindy reminded herself, this would all entail more ireful parents, infuriated adults, and probably other indignant people at their school as well. In case Kathy tried to call the police or anyone, Cathy would convince her otherwise, at least for tonight.

Navarro halted his Bronco at a red light. They were a block away from Kathy's house.

Navarro turned toward Cindy to try and engage her again in conversation.

Cindy saw him looking at her. She realized that he was probably dispirited. She reminded herself that she had not thanked him yet for the ride.

Somehow though, with the events of the evening swimming about in her thoughts—the argument with her father at the restaurant, the weird tackiness of her friend's misadventures at the motel—Cindy wanted to forget everything, push it all away.

Cindy sidled nearer to Navarro. When he turned to look at her again, she placed her lips to his.

The suddenness of Cindy's advance startled Navarro. He let her kiss him until his mind caught up with his body and then kissed her back.

Cindy knew that Navarro's sense of dejection had dissipated.

She felt herself becoming lighter. So close to him, Navarro's boyish attar inundated her nose, comforting her.

Before they began to neck in earnest, they were interrupted by a honk behind them.

The light had flipped to green some time ago.

Cindy saw Navarro trying not to smile too much. He stopped idling his car and drove her to her friend's house.

In front of Kathy's home, Navarro made a move toward Cindy, but she deflected away from him coquettishly.

—See you tomorrow! She laughed.

Cindy jumped down from the Bronco and scampered indoors.

Closing the door behind her, she peered back through the door's glass panel.

She watched as Navarro drove away.

If they were to become an item, Cindy thought, then she was going to have to make him fix the seatbelts in his car.

Oils

No morning romp, no private onanism; no shared breakfast, no quick snack; no pot of coffee, no shot of espresso: the two hours or so before dawn had to be used for work, had to be used solely for painting.

Sevek awoke because of despair. But he awoke quietly, disturbing neither Pranaya nor the child sleeping bodkin between her parents. His wife and daughter knew nothing of his desperation. They only had a vague sense of his plight, understood that he wanted to paint, but did not know the ultimate reason why.

Pranaya's head lay unpillowed. She was as supine to her husband's plight as she was to the world beyond their mattress.

Sevek's daughter, lying flesh against her mother's umber midriff, seemed lifeless to him. Both the females looked dead in their sleep.

The painter rolled away from his family toward the uncurtained window. The city glow of downtown Dallas murmured into the bedroom, enough to allow Sevek to read the timepiece at the other end of their bedroom. He had some time yet ere dawn.

Not a fear of failure, but a fear of having no evidence of his existence motivated him to rustle himself from bed. If he had had friends who were composers or writers or directors, he would have inquired into the muses that spark their creations.

Sevek's sense was that struggle was the raison d'etre for any self-aware artist. He did not care if this reflection was bromidic. The reason was real and impassioned.

He despised the fight though, the artist's fight, hated it with all his material being, wanted to choke his drive to create, drown the resilience underwater, like pushing his own daughter's rubicund face into a shallow spring puddle—if only it were so easy? This was how he defined his desperation: unwanted, yet warranted.

Sevek willed himself into the adjoining room whither his canvases, oils, and brushes lay scattered about. Most of his paraphernalia had been relegated to a single corner of their one-bedroom loft by Pranaya, but evidence of Sevek's industry rarely stayed confined to that ignoble spot. These days, empty paint tubes and headless brushes could be found intermingled with their toddler's playthings.

He pulled the switch to the incandescent lamp and was startled to see a man sleeping on their vintage Bauhaus.

Sevek forgot that his wife's younger brother had come up from college for an interview in Pranaya's company. He was to interview today. He would probably get the position, Sevek guessed, become another Indian twiddling away his existence in the American IT sector. He would later become naturalized like Pranaya.

Sevek scoffed, which was more the cliché in America: he the milksop artist-painter struggling with his middle-class angst or his brother-in-law the Indian-runaway struggling to become another computer code wallah in the West? Even though Sevek did not have to fret over finances because of Pranaya's career—instead he enjoyed a much more expensive lifestyle than he ever would have in India—he disliked being associated with its stereotypes.

The brother-in-law had not been disturbed by the sallow light. Sevek spotted some early-morning dribble at the corner of his lips. Some saliva stuck to Sevek's sofa, some onto the student's University of North Texas tee-shirt. The collegiate green of his shirt hurt Sevek's eyes. Out of consideration, Sevek turned the lamp off.

Sevek retreated to his corner in the dark, soon realizing that he could not paint with so little luminescence. He looked back through the open door into his bedroom, onto the figures of his wife and child.

Dim urban light limned their persons.

Sevek, feeling the tingle of inspiration, quickly grabbed at a mounted sheet of canvas, some brushes, painter's apron, and his thin, light-weight easel. He deposited these painter's accoutrements near the bedroom window.

He returned for his oils but recalled that he had used the last of his turpentine the previous morning. Acrylics were an option; they required only water for thinning. But Sevek already knew that he was not about to use those amateurish things: once an oil painter, always an oil painter. He opted for oil sticks instead: the smaller pastels from Japan, the larger cattle-markers from his new host country.

From the dull streetlamps outside, all the multifarious colors and hues—columned next to each other in their case like bars on a grill plate—appeared only monochromatic.

He chose one of the darker shades and struck oil to canvas.

Sevek was experienced; he knew never to let a blank canvas intimidate him: better to slash at the airy, affronting glare of the canvas' bald face, then to wait for an unlikely rencontre between canvas and painter. Before looking at a subject, Sevek's hand was always at work.

Sevek started to trace the body's line.

He had sketched his wife's profile numerous times

when they were younger, but recounted that he had not done so since the birth of their daughter. Pranaya refused to sit for him anymore. This was a punishment, a punishment for Sevek for being more of a servant to his drawings than to his family.

Before their daughter's appearance, Pranaya had found her husband's otiose behavior charming, his artsy inclinations romantic; she had nurtured these, much as she nurtured her daughter now. But with new responsibility had come a new reality. Sevek's inability to sell paintings had become a superfluity, his inability to provide income unacceptable.

She was the breadwinner, he admitted freely. But Sevek did not like to cogitate over these facts often. They depressed him. He only wanted to paint.

Pranaya had turned over on her side. Even as she slept, her countenance was hard, like one of those bronze statues that always seem to face the wind. Her night slip had loosened and the side of her right breast had become visible. The comforter had been kicked away hours ago because of the heat; the air conditioner was never a match for the sultry summer air in Dallas. All that was draped over her and her daughter's body was a thin cotton sheet.

Sevek was surprised how much he enjoyed using the oil pastels.

He had always considered these sticks of color a lesser art to the brush, but the quick movement and interchange between the rods of color was liberating. If he had had any turpentine left, he would have experimented with dipping the sticks into the solution. He pondered upon using linseed oil from the kitchen, and was about to retrieve some, when, on the nightstand, he espied a bottle of baby oil, capturing the streetlights like old-fashioned isinglass.

Sevek squeezed the remaining contents of the bottle

onto a plate. Dunking one of the pastels into the gooey oil, he applied the wetted stick to the canvas. The color shot across the cloth.

He laughed: the struggle seemed today more playful than it had in years. Using the oil pastels in place of the brush reminded him that he should experiment oftener.

When he heard the downtown Spanish market below coming alive, Sevek knew his productivity would soon wane, giving on to the waking family. He added a few more stokes to the canvass, then left the easel stand —picture facing the window's growing sunlight—and returned to bed. Slumber embraced him quickly.

A cacophony of domestication awoke Sevek an hour later: an irate wife was grumbling, a shower was warming up, a child was oozing snot, a television was relaying something unintelligible, a spoiled bother-in-law was smacking his lips over breakfast, a phone was ringing. Sevek surrendered to the forces propelling him forward and rolled out of bed for a second time.

—When are you going to answer the phone? Sevek asked when he saw his wife and brother-in-law around the kitchen table. His daughter was strapped into a highchair, slapping a plastic cup against one of its sides.

—When are you going to clean up that mess in our bedroom? Pranaya shot back.

She reached over to the landline.

—Hello? Ohh! Papa! *Kya kar rahe ho, papa-ji?*

Pranaya laughed into the receiver.

—I am missing you too! *Kya?* Oh, you saw on the news? No no, the tornado didn't come through here. It went through Ft. Worth. No no, it's next to Dallas, but not the same city. What time is it in Delhi? Oh, not so late. You are wanting to talk to your son, I know!! Okay okay, love you!

Pranaya handed the phone off to her younger brother, who began chirping away in Hindi. Ignoring her husband, Pranaya moved past him into the bedroom shower. Sevek had no job to run off to, so he was in no rush to bathe, eat, or compose himself for anything that involved the outside world.

On seeing her father, Sevek's daughter smiled, clapped her hands, and then banged her cup a few more times before dropping it to the floor. Losing her plastic cup came as something of a shock to the child. She cried.

—Sevek! Can you watch her, please!! I don't have time for this this morning, Pranaya yelled from shower.

Sevek did as he was told and reached out for his two-year-old. The girl wailed harder. Not sure how to appease the blubbering creature, Sevek bumbled about the kitchen looking for something to satiate her. Looks of ill-will from his brother-in-law on the phone convinced him to take his daughter into their bedroom.

After placing her on the bed, Sevek remembered his pastels. He took hold of the set he had used earlier along with some unpaid bills and yellowing receipts towering atop their dresser and set them in front of the child. The rows of colors were even more majestic in the morning sunlight. His daughter was enchanted. Her father smiled.

Pranaya returned from her shower, two towels wrapped around her. Though having lived in America for ten years, she still preferred to keep her tresses as long as her cousins did back on the subcontinent. As his wife dressed, Sevek followed the wispy movement of black sheen, like a tomcat eyeing a dangling string.

—What are you doing? I said watch her. Not be letting her draw all over our sheets! Pranaya's chided her husband in a Hindi-accented English with a penchant for the present progressive tense.

Her voice rent Sevek's playful voyeurism.

—She's okay. She's not drawing on the sheets.

The child had long since strayed from the few paltry pieces of paper onto the linen. Sevek guided his daughter's hands back to the papers.

Pranaya began searching through her many containers and instruments of feminine beauty and apparel.

—Have you seen the baby oil?

—Yeah, I've got it. It's over here. I was using it earlier this morning.

—Using it for what?

—For painting.

Pranaya sighed:

—Is there any left?

Sevek moved to where his easel was still standing. He retrieved the plastic bottle from the stand and gave the container a squeeze. Wheezy air escaped but no oil.

—Can't you be a little more considerate? She accosted him. What is your daughter supposed to use now? You already waste enough money on your paints and brushes. And now you have to be taking from your own daughter?

Pranaya clicked her tongue in triumphal conclusion.

If it was for their daughter, then why was Pranaya using it, Sevek was about to retort, but he held his tongue.

He got up and went to the canvass. He picked up what was left of the baby oil, and, upon attempting to return the bottle to his wife, tripped on a leg of the easel. The canvas was jarred easily from the stand and slipped to the carpeted floor, picture side up.

Pranaya looked down at the painting. Sevek stopped to take in the image, too. The colors he had chosen before dawn, when all he had was the faint municipal glow of urbanization, now blazed prismaticaly under the riled strength of the naked Texas sun. The stroke and glide of the oil sticks had culminated to produce a lively stillness, like movement caught under a slow-shuttering camera. The composition was unevenly balanced so that the final image of slumbering mother and child was tensely calm. Sevek had been able to capture the image of a fitful sleeper fallen into a deep sleep, and a child grabbing at a cosmos of exploding stars in her imagination. He had documented an edgy serenity in the form of two slumbering figures.

Sevek caught the movement of his daughter in his periphery. She was teetering over the side of the yard-high mattress, trying to follow the gaze of her mother and father.

She lost her balance.

—Rangasaz! Her father called.

Sevek caught his daughter before she hit the floor.

Pranaya turned away from her husband's painting to see him holding little Rangasaz. She looked back the painting.

—Sevek, maybe this one's alright.

The Gulf

Having that view of the gulf was important to the retired high school instructor. New apartments had been built, a modern shopping boulevard had been developed, and, even, a row of storage units had been constructed over the decades, but that view—his own private vantage point onto the salt water that seeps into Galveston, Texas every day—that view had been maintained.

Old Man Rockwall Darby sat on his favorite stiff-backed chair, his one arm dangling over the rainswept balcony railing, the other in his lap. He absorbed the open emptiness and friendly loneliness of having lived too long, a feeling somehow calmed by the vastness of his view onto the Gulf of Mexico. No breeze comforted him off the waters this morning, only the warm reflection of a listless sun.

A sound of crick-crackling gravel and then the purring down of an engine robbed his attention from the sea. This was followed by the sound of footsteps on a hollow wooden stair ramp, and then an opening and closing of a door. The weighty footsteps casually made their way through the two-story house and then onto the balcony.

Rockwall looked up. He winced at the appearance of his son.

The org, Rockwall thought to himself.

If his wife were still alive, he would have quipped

something about the bumptious gigantism of her side of the family. His son's stature always startled him.

Father did not rise to embrace son, nor did son bother to greet father.

The young adult instead glanced down at his paterfamilias and wondered how something so frail and thinly could have seeded something as barreling as himself. The only child, not born until Rockwall was already in his later forties, the twenty-year-old understood that his existence probably amounted to a faulty prophylactic more than anything.

The son raised his eyes from the pensioner, settling his gaze on the oceanic view that his father had just been pondering.

Rockwall approved. The expansive turn of the silver-wet horizon should never be slighted—a worn-down teacher, yes, that can be ignored—but the view he had clung to his whole adult life, no, that deserved reverence.

Rockwall noticed the twelve-pack of Mexican-branded beer in his kin's hand.

The father sighed and said:

—I haven't had my coffee yet.

Rockwall's son turned his back on the gulf and leant against the railing. Removing the bottle opener attached to his car keys from his front pocket, he opened two bottles without responding.

The retiree took his beer.

The young man drank half the auburn bottle's contents in a gulp. A relaxed grin spread across his countenance.

—I wanted to celebrate, the son spoke.

Rockwall's gaze was back onto the water.

—I wanted to celebrate because Joanne is pregnant.

The son laughed.

—And I think I'm going to name the kid Rockwall. Even though it's a terrible first name for a boy, if it is a boy I mean, I'm going to name him Rockwall.

The soon-to-be-father downed his cerveza and opened a second.

In the distance, silhouetted birds hovered about silently. Rockwall stopped counting them. The expansive waters were still sacred, that was no was no question. But now he breathed freedom and release and eternity all at once as only an apostate can.

The retired school teacher smiled and asked his son for another bottle.

Drywall

Head Coach Patterson leant into the crowbar, heaving his weight against the bar of iron until the drywall loosened slowly before yawing open. Flecks of chalky plaster clouded the stillness of the small, emptied-out bedroom. Wiping the sweat from his brow with the back of his arm, the man walked to the window and released the latch to slide open a pane of glass. Patterson looked up from the second floor of his newly bought house to see the stadium of Southern Methodist University. Thoughts of the previous weekend's soccer game loss were rekindled.

Below a crash, a yell, and then some laughing sounded through the house.

Patterson could hear his wife's voice reprimanding their two daughters.

He laughed as well, wondering what the girls had broken. The sound had reverberated from the kitchen, through the halls, and up to the second floor. The coach hoped they were making him lunch.

Again Patterson doubted whether purchasing the fifty-year-old house was sensible. He liked that he could walk to work, to his locker-room offices, and visit home during the lunch hours, maybe see more of his elementary-aged daughters. But the house had many problems.

With attempting to save money by making modifications himself, his free time was being chiseled away with remodeling. The coach was already regretting promising his wife that he could expand their bedroom.

Patterson surveyed the destruction he had wrought thus far. He admitted that he would need to incur the cost of real carpenter at some point—but not today.

The coach could not help looking at the stadium again. The complex appeared more monolithic than it really was, overbearing from his vantage point.

On fortuitous weekends, when Patterson was able to command the varsity team toward a win, then the architectural tribune of tubular metal and blocked concrete was a welcoming sight, a triumph to victory. On weekends like the last, the building never escaped his view, suffocating his mood every time he dared turn toward a window. Every glassed orifice of his house offered a perspective onto the terrible structure.

Leaving the window, the coach brandished the hook end of the bar, hovering the iron in the air as if it were a bat.

Patterson swung violently at the wall. Bracing his foot against the crumbling plasterboard, he pulled at the crowbar recklessly. Too much leverage caused the man to place his foot through the aged wall. Losing his balance, he fell awkwardly, slipping to the floor. The crowbar, with a sizeable chunk of drywall, fell with him, showering the coach with a thousand snow-white particles of plaster.

Picking himself up peevishly, Patterson espied his daughters staring at him blankly from the door.

The older girl held a bologna sandwich in her hand, the younger cupping a glass of water carefully so as not to drop it.

—Daddy, you're white! his youngest yelped.

The girls giggled.

Patterson shook his head, shoulders, and body, spattering the room with dried plaster.

The girls screamed playfully, running away from the flying specks.

—What are you two laughing at, their mother asked, halting them at the end of the hall and turning them back around to the room.

—Pat, the girls have your lunch. We have one more beer left in the fridge from…

The coach's wife stopped speaking when she saw her husband.

When she started to laugh, the girls followed.

—You look like a black ghost.

Patterson smiled:

—Honey, I'd love a beer.

The Bat Mitzvah

Outside, rain prattled upon the panes of glass protecting the adolescents from an otherwise frosty reality. The children were playing grownup: they were having a party, their reason for celebration a blond girl's bat mitzvah.

An unseasonable inclemency was murmuring about in downtown Houston, Texas, wetting the street and sidewalk until they glowed like neon from the warm lighting inside the café.

Most of the boys at the party cared very little for dancing.

A large contingency of emotionally riled girls, however, excited the evening air inside the small, rented-out restaurant with an urgency that finally riled the boys into action as well: odd avatars for this singular evening, their twelve- and thirteen-year-old male bodies charged forward, finding mates for another slow song.

The girls delighted whenever their person was chosen. Even the young females who were unable to receive their preferred dancing partner, these girls too felt a chill of excitement when invited onto the floor.

Sweaty hands and mint-sweetened breaths radiated extra warmth.

The heaters were unnecessary at this point, though still turned on. Everywhere was warmth, everywhere was gaily nervous smiles, everywhere a sense for the children on the parquetry floor that this evening was magical, that they would remember it always, that they were reaching toward some happy acme.

To fool oneself into the transcendence of the moment was to fool oneself into the uniqueness therein: all the youths felt this majesty of emotion, all touched it, all tasted is—that is, all but one.

One boy knew something of the chill outside.

An adult coughed gravely as he rustled himself quickly indoors, a biting jet of outside cold following him.

Closing the outside door, this chaperon saw Htoo Wah set aside from the rest of the group.

Htoo Wah was new to the area.

He and his family had recently been resettled to Houston. They had attained refugee status and been shipped over from the mountains that separate Thailand and Myanmar to the suburbs outside Houston before the start of fall.

Watching Htoo Wah, the adult smiled to himself; he liked that there was one child who had not yet sallied forward in search of a mate. Maybe because he was a shy, single man himself, he wanted to succor this forlorn-looking youth.

Htoo Wah watched the strange scene before him. He did not feel prepared for the evening.

Htoo Wah's borrowed sports jacket, dark-dark blue with affected gold buttons, his drab cinnabar tie, and his ill-fitting oxford shirt: all were uncomfortable and scratchy. He wore jeans for his bottom half. His father had commented on his pants before Htoo Wah left for the party, agreeing that Americans always wore jeans, thus his son would be just as handsome as all the other American boys at the reception party.

When Htoo Wah's ride had arrived, Tom and Charlene, the father-mother couple coming to pick him up, had shot each other looks of disapproval after espying the child's ratty jeans and colorful sneakers, especially since they had just finished an argument with their own son on the impropriety of not donning slacks with a blazer.

But, he was just a refugee, was he not? The native couple had pondered. Htoo Wah and his family would still need time to understand.

Htoo Wah felt someone watching him. He turned toward the affronting person.

The middle-aged adult walked toward him. The man's gait was timid.

Htoo Wah's first thought on seeing this chaperon was that his father could easily fight him, strike him to the ground with one forward kickboxing kick. The adult's tie was as tawny as Htoo Wah's, but more floral. His hair was unstylishly cropped short.

The adult coughed:

—Not gonna do any dancing? The man questioned Htoo Wah cheerfully.

The boy did not understand him.

English was a problem. Though, of course, the adult's cosmopolitanized Texan accent would not have been easy for any foreigner new to English, Htoo Wah was still completely lost.

How much more time would he need before he would not always have to play the mute, Htoo Wah wondered—before he could engage anyone on any topic easily?

Htoo Wah smiled faintly.

The adult spoke again:

—See lots of nice ladies out there; no reason to be playing the wallflower, now is there?

Again the thirteen-year-old was dismayed.

Htoo Wah followed the adult's gestures to where the

klatch of adolescents was careening to the last slow beats of the last slow song. He surmised correctly that the adult wanted him to join the others.

As the tune twilighted, decrescendoing into a black blanket of quiet naught, the girls broke with their partners and buzzed toward each other to form their own maleless group. They traded whispery secrets and giggles.

Again the disc jockey began another slow song. Worried that their boyish counterparts might quit the dance floor entirely, the schoolgirls disbanded quickly, presenting themselves for the next dance.

Htoo Wah watched as the blond Jewish girl was first to be partnered by one of the braver boys. The boy, like himself, was clothed in a jacket, button-down shirt, and maroon tie. He, too, was wearing jeans for his bottom. Htoo Wah recognized the brand of the boy's jeans—knew that they cost almost as much as his family received from social services every month.

—Better hurry on up! The adult encouraged Htoo Wah.

If he was going to have to dance, Htoo Wah wanted to couple with the blond girl. She was the most beautiful of the girls, he thought. Though no wild tempos beat or syncopated rhythms jostled, everyone had made space for her and her partner's languid swaying.

Htoo Wah knew, vaguely, who she was, knew that she was the center of the evening's celebrations, but had neither learnt her name nor ever even taken notice of her before tonight.

Htoo Wah's middle school housed three thousand students, most of them Caucasian, most of the girls as bright-faced and blond as the Jewess reigning in the middle of the group. Her ubiquity for Htoo Wah, then, was beyond reproach.

The disc jockey's lighting equipment scintillated pleasantly, projecting off the silver-topped bar, the glassy tabletops, and the calcimined ceiling. Outside the café, the darkened sky promised that nothing of the streets would be visible to those inside. All that the attendees recognized when they looked through the restaurant's wide-paneled windows were their own merry reflections.

The adult's sleeveless advice was unacknowledged by Htoo Wah. The man recognized that he was not reaching the boy. He tried again:

—Guess they don't do much dancing where you come from. Where are you from? Thailand, raight? Tom and Charlene mentioned something of the sort.

The adult wondered if maybe the boy did not understand him.

Verily, Htoo Wah caught one word from the shovel of syntax being dumped on him: Thailand! The boy spotted this word easily. Now Htoo Wah could respond:

—I no from Thailan', I from Myanmar country, no Thailan'.

Htoo Wah read the perplexity on the adult's face.

—"Myanmar"? the man uttered blankly, trying to cudgel his brain as to where he might have heard that word.

Myanmar sounded familiar, vaguely recognizable, like some fact the man may have learnt back in college, some trivial nothing that was easily forgotten as the years dribbled on. When Tom and Charlene had retold their story to others—their good deed for the evening, visiting Htoo Wah's family to pick him up, including the new refugee boy in the activities of his classmates—the man had had a point of reference for Thailand. Though he did not know exactly where Thailand would be painted on a world map, he had recounted the curiosa-like story of a colleague of his at the company: something to do with elephants tromping next to skyscrapers and fellatio for under twenty dollars. He had even pondered wrangling his own bachelor self over to Thailand one day—but Myanmar?

Htoo Wah acknowledged the glazed look that gleaned over the chaperon's eyes. Three months of similarly confused countenances of his school-aged peers had trained the boy that more explanation was necessary:

—I from Burma country. Burma country is Myanmar country. I from Karen State.

Pride etched its way onto the surface of Htoo Wah's voice when he said the word Karen, the title of his ethic group.

The man said the word Karen to himself as well, though he pronounced it with the stress on the first syllable, anglicizing the disyllable so that it resembled a female name.

Htoo Wah again recognized the futility of attempting any palaver in English.

Htoo Wah suddenly began feeling sorry himself, wishing that the strange couple, the young-looking father-mother duo of Tom and Charlene, had not shown up at their apartment to whisk him away. Htoo Wah wished that he could have friends like he had once had in the mountaintop refugee camp, friends who understood him, friends to joke and jibe and play.

Across the room from Htoo Wah, a pudgy girl, juicy with anticipation, was having her own trouble attracting a partner.

The girl was trying not to eye the crowd, feigning her best sangfroid, but her desire to be chosen by a boy, any boy, was steamy, like vapor spiriting off a hot ironing board. Having won two partners out of the last three dances, the girl was nervous to relive the short, but exactingly cool, burn of having to stand aside for even one song.

The dumpy girl envied her blond friend, who always seemed to find a partner.

Making their chaperoning rounds, Tom and Charlene flittered past the girl.

Charlene's appetency for banal benevolence was insatiable. Eying the girl, Charlene was not going to let one of the youths stumble by the wayside—no matter what her waist size. Charlene surmised the teenager's straits with a glance:

—Who is that boy over there? Charlene's soft voice slithered.

The thirteen-year-old girl swiveled her corpulent head, following the gaze of her elder until her eyes spotted Htoo Wah. The Asian boy was in her pre-algebra class. Korean?—she tried to recount to herself—though not Korean-American, surely. He was still too foreign, not quite cool enough to deserve the "American" suffix yet.

The girl surveyed her mass of peers. She gave up waiting to be invited again and moved toward Htoo Wah and the middle-aged man.

Another good deed tallied for the evening, Charlene moved on, Tom in tow.

Htoo Wah and the older gentleman noticed the larger girl at the same moment.

Whilst the man smiled, recognizing an opportunity for the youth he was trying to aid, Htoo Wah's face was statuesque, bereft of anything friendly or otherwise.

The girl's eagerness to return to the center of floor with a partner grew as she neared them.

The older chaperon nudged Htoo Wah forward.

Htoo Wah also suddenly felt the zephyrs of opportunity. He knew that he was about to engage in rituals he had skirted until now.

The new slow song was starting. Panic lighted the hefty girl's eyes, exhilaration Htoo Wah's.

—Pre-Algebra kind of sucks, the girl forwarded by way of greeting.

Htoo Wah wanted to respond, but did not know how.

—Yeah, so, anyway...like let's dance. Y'all have slow dancing in Korea, right?

The older man gave Htoo Wah the last nudge he would require for the evening.

The girl led him by hand onto the fey dance floor.

She placed her forearms as elegantly as she could over the boy's shoulders, clasping her hands together behind his neck.

His own arms dangling at his sides, Htoo Wah stood stupidly until the girl broke her stance to maneuver his hands over her midriff.

—No, like this. This is how we do it in Texas.

Htoo Wah looked around him for clues to decipher the girl's utterances.

All the other teenage boys had their arms around their partners. He saw that the blond girl and her boy held onto each other very closely.

With Htoo Wah's own partner guiding his nervous arms around the middle part of her body, he fought through bewilderment and brought the chubby frame of his dance partner closer to his. Unlike the other boys who were able to reach their arms around their partner's body easily, Htoo Wah managed only to hook the ends of his index fingers behind the girl's broad back.

—So how long you've been in Texas? You know, I've been to Korea before. Yeah, my dad's in the Navy, so we had to live on base for some time. I've had Korean friends before too. You know, you look like one of the singers in Shinee. Has anyone ever told you that? But you're more tanned though.

Concentrating on the moment, trying to keep his arms locked together around her, watching others to learn what to do, avoiding as best he could becoming tonight's reigning sad sack, Htoo Wah did not understand anything the girl said. All he knew was that, whether from far away or from up close, his partner was the most unattractive girl at the party.

Though the song was listlessly slow, the blond Jewess constantly swirled about.

Htoo Wah traced her and her partner's glowing wake. When they whirled past Htoo Wah and his larger companion, her eyes, star-like, locked with Htoo Wah's. The azure blue of her pupils reminded him of glazed candies. She allowed him a smile, and then seemed to disappear before nearing back toward where Htoo Wah and his girl were lamely swaying.

Close enough to bump shoulders, Htoo Wah's plump partner leant in to say something to the blonde. Exchanging smiles, they giggled.

—You're Korean? The blond girl asked him.

The two couples were now very close to each other; the rest of the dance floor revolved around their axis.

—I from Karen State, from Burma country. No Korea country, Htoo Wah replied airily, but confidently so.

His words were lost in the exciting rabble of another changing of jockeyed music, and thus another change of partners.

The blond girl's partner cast Htoo Wah a confronting glance. As the music changed, he made no movement to let go of his prize, but the twelve-year-old girl had already decided to break with the boy, at least for the time being. She too had noticed his acid-wet glance in Htoo Wah's direction. She pushed her partner's arms from her light frame with hauteur and grabbed at Htoo Wah.

The evening's most important girl led Htoo Wah away from his fattier partner and to a new area of the dance floor, nearer to the speakers, nearer to where the middle-aged man who had been trying to converse with him earlier had stood.

The party-smarts of an adult society girl funneled through the blonde's arteries and veins, circulating through her system, feeding all five levels of her brain with more than just oxygen. Though born into that oddly North American, and uniquely ubiquitous middle-middle-class stratification of society, something impelled the girl to think herself unjustly caged amidst the ragged ruins of poverty. She would never learn that having a mother, honest and quiet, who was also a primary school teacher, and a father, sober and dependable, who was also a deep-water-drilling geologist might be seen as something of a success story for the majority of her species. She executed her worldview beauteously and always without any hiccup of her accidently discovering her essential meaningless for the rest of our ever-expanding universe.

All eyes were now pinned upon the freshest couple massaging the wooden floor with their shuffling feet: the party's main girl and the unknown boy.

The blonde was ecstatic about the attention she was garnering. This was a sensation!

Htoo Wah, too, though beyond the comfortableness of his usually inhibited self, felt the excitement of being one of two foci.

When Htoo Wah surveyed the youths and chaperoning adults from his new loftier position, he had difficulty seeing beyond the dazzling lights and translucent colors and shiny nothings that bedazzled his retina.

Someone had opened the restaurant's back door, so

that a stream or two of clean, autumn air might jet about the rafters of the downtown establishment. The nastiness of the weather outside stood no chance against the moist warmness of glee inside. Instead, the nighttime air only enlivened the youths.

An extra urgency seemed to fall from the air above them. The spell fell to the floor, before settling like invisible stardust amongst the tapping toes and hovering heels of the youths. Every shuffle of foot or slide of gait caused some of the magic to stir up into the spaces between their bodies. The youths breathed in the dusty elixir with every breath.

Htoo Wah recognized a few of his classmates.

He knew none of their names, only their bright white faces. Htoo Wah spotted the couple, Tom and Charlene, who had ferried him here to this party. He saw their son, his face following Htoo Wah and the blond girl's movements jealously. He espied the middle-aged man who had talked to him earlier, the sorry gentleman standing alone, off to one side. Htoo Wah then betook the countenance of the blonde's previous dance partner. The boy scowled at him with envious contumely, genuine and viperously green.

The blonde did not engage in conversation with Htoo Wah. Her interests lay elsewhere.

Htoo Wah did not want to talk either, so he let the music surround him and his dancing partner. He was happy to inspect the girl in front of him.

Her slim pulchritude, her trumpery accessories that jingled as much as they glittered, her yellowish tresses, sometimes seemingly flaxen, other times nearly neon from the disco lights—everything visual about the young lady was consumed by Htoo Wah's searching spirit. She was not as talkative as his erstwhile dancing heifer had been. Htoo Wah sensed that this girl would be the harder won catch if ever he would have to compete for the two.

Again Htoo Wah took in all that surrounded him in the middle of the restaurant's small dance floor.

He ruminated on the expressions hidden behind all those who stared at him now. Some displayed bewilderment; he understood that. Others seemed to offer encouragement. Others still vivified an earnest disbelief.

After returning his glance to the figure before him— braving a direct purview into the girl's eyes—his thoughts stumbled upon a harsh lesson: she was as uninterested in him as he had been in his last partner.

He was being used.

There was no enigma here; another brief glimpse at the unkind countenance of the blond girl's last budding consort revealed her larger scheme.

Instead of fretting, feeling any anger, or partaking of a round of jealousy on his own part, Htoo Wah felt relieved. Whether or not the blonde liked him was inconsequential; he had neither ever entertained such a thought nor wished it true. What barreled through his thoughts was a remembrance of who he really was, who he really had been before he had landed in modern suburbia.

Htoo Wah recounted his last two years in the jungle-forested refugee camp along the Thai-Burmese border.

Atop those misty mountains, hidden amidst the backward politics of misanthropic régimes and incompetent agencies, buried beneath months of soppy rainy seasons and tropical summers, surrounded by sordid hardships that should have died out from our species long ago—atop all of those otherworldly dreams—Htoo Wah remembered all the friends he had once had.

He remembered scenes where village girls would flirt with him and mud-bedraggled boys would play-fight with him.

He relived the times when their own Karen tribe had had dances: the coquettish moves with their suggestive jerks and lurks and shakes, the playful rhythms espoused with every deflecting flinch of hand, jostle of midriff, or slide of chin.

He remembered a life where he had been esteemed.

Htoo Wah felt emboldened.

Unlike any other twelve- or thirteen-year-old boys present, he pulled the waist of the blonde flush up against his own person.

The girl, startled, ceased forwarding attention toward her last partner.

Htoo Wah smiled at her.

Though the blonde wanted to pull back, she could not—not because this boy's grip was unbreachable, but because she could not make herself.

Htoo Wah again glanced up from his companion, this time catching the eye of the middle-aged bachelor who had tried to befriend him earlier.

Htoo Wah compared the man to his own father for the second time that evening.

He knew that his patriarch was thinner, smaller in stature, less bulky all around, but Htoo Wah recognized immediately that there was something tangibly missing from this other man when compared to his father. Some strength of will was wanting: a grief-bedight wretchedness limned the middle-aged man's person as completely as it did his persona.

Htoo Wah imagined his father ripping through the man, wreaking completely the spirit and body of this nobody. At this moment, Htoo Wah knew as completely as he had ever known anything, that whatever womanish path had led to what befouled this miserable man, whatever that dreary deniability was, that that was something which would never pollute him.

Htoo Wah's life, his venturing out beyond his own fears, out beyond the refugee camp, out beyond the safety of his parent's home, would waylay any impertinent obstacle.

Htoo Wah would never wait to be asked to dance again.

Across the room the man timorously proffered a thumbs-up to Htoo Wah.

Airfare

Peter noticed that every blocky pillar shielded sunlight. The atmosphere in DFW Airport Terminal D
felt more like the staleness of a dentist's office than
the international showcase the untraveled architects had
envisioned.

Peter watched as some kids, three blond-haired imps,
ran past him.

The children tussled and chased each other from one
structural column to another. Apathetic to the jet-setting
passengers ambulating swiftly from port of arrival to port
of departure, the oldest amidst the careless bunch of children laughed when one of his peerage tackled him, tum-
bling all three to the glassy-waxed linoleum floor. The
children's reflection was doubled so close to the floor: their
persons, though somewhat blurred, now counted six.

The smallest of the band of siblings stood to induct
another round of roughhousing, but caught her plastic
sandal in the jacket of her older brother, causing her to
slip suddenly as if she were a hoofed creature on ice. The
girl slapped her pate against the glass wall dividing the
inside of the terminal to the early morning summer sky
outside. The four-year-old caterwauled, her scream rent-
ing the otherwise uneventful air around them all.

A mother, clothed in some sort of aerobics gear better
suited for the gym than for an outside world where her
duds belied more than just apathy for personal appear-

ance, rushed to the little girl.

When the trailer-park matriarch leant down to proffer womanly anodyne to her blubbering snot-bedight kin, an ass crack as unblanketed as the Rio Grande Valley that separates Texas from Mexico broke free from her neon pink—hot, hyper hot pink—sweats. She showered the passing world with an acme of beauteously unrehearsed lower-middleclass banality.

Peter, gripping his carryon on the slowly rolling conveyor belt, winced when the mother's naked display affronted what had been a picture-perfect archetype of merry youth, now soured into something tearfully tacky. He wished the rubbery walking-belt would accelerate, whisk him to his departure gate more quickly.

A snowy-sallow Asiatic couple pushed passed him rudely on the level walkway.

Chinese from mainland, not Taiwanese, Peter ruminated as saw them slither along faster than the horizontal escalator did. He pinpointed them as of the majority Han ethnicity, maybe from Beijing, though more likely residents of Tianjin.

The Han woman espied the same disastrously viewable buttocks that Peter had just seen.

Not catching everything the woman said to her disinterested husband in Mandarin, Peter was happy enough to understand at least the following:

—Fat American pig.

Like being velcroed, always, to one of a thousand different world cultures—sometimes stuck to this land, sometimes latched onto that culture—Peter, at the machinegun rhythm of the Northern Chinese's dialect, felt his strip of velcro already beginning to unfurl from the North American continent.

Peter knew that there is no better drug of release from

the pedestrian existence of one's own upbringing than the intellectual rewards that are promised from having mastered another language in adulthood. Feeling aglow, he began planning what new language he ought to tackle next. This upcoming assignment in Japan would give him an opportunity.

Peter could already taste the sovereignty of spirit—that nomadic freedom—that is intimately bound up with travel. Though no new beginnings were being foretold for the man, nothing that he had not experienced a hundred times before, Peter still felt the exciting release of knowing one is about to grab at another opportunity of forsaking their boyhood homeland, dropping it like bag of moldy laundry.

Is there any greater sin for an Texas-born American than admitting that there is a world outside of their country, Peter pondered, and that one feels more at home in this world? He felt less like the prodigal with every step closer to his departure gate and more like himself with every step farther away from his motherland.

Peter exited the motorized walkway to review the marquee. He sighed when he saw that his flight was delayed; the jet would not depart for another three and a half hours.

He should have just paid the extra half of a grand, eschewing the connecting flight altogether. Even though the voyage was on the company, he had chosen the cheaper airfare to save on his project's expenses. Instead of a simple Houston-to-Narita departing on time, he would now have to wait for a Houston-to-Vancouver, Vancouver-to-Narita that was tardy. He mulled over the possibility of switching his air ticket.

Peter's attention was again arrested by the homely mother and her rambunctious children. They came rambling down the corridor like a group of brain-diseased monkeys. The woman's presence in particular soiled his mood.

Peter charged to the nearest ticket counter and changed his flight to the non-stop Houston-to-Narita. When asked if he would like to exchange his miles for an upgrade to first class, Peter's response issued forth from deepest recesses of his soul:

—For heaven's sake, woman! Yes!

W Martin Luther King Jr Blvd

Leaning his back against the side of his boxy-shaped Lincoln, Scott Ehrlich peered inside the authentically inauthentic Mexican restaurant. The atmosphere inside was fuggy. Too late for the lunch crowd, too early for average diners, the only people inside the corner-side establishment were a few predictable seniors. Scott wondered how much longer he would have to wait for his friend's shift to finish.

The young man's eyes rested on a hoary Mestizo couple dining inside. Like jam sliding down the curved side of a glass jar, black refried beans suddenly dribbled from the side of the old man's mouth, which his wife reached over to wipe away. Her deftness attested to her having performed this rescue act before—as well as to her resignation of her partner's physical ineptitudes.

Scott ruminated on old age, but not for long; to do so would have been as useless as the old recounting what it was like to have been young.

Espying another person across the charcoal-gray parking lot—a comrade of his in that this petite woman also seemed to be waiting for someone to get off work—Scott envied the cigarette in her fingers. Something about her told him that she was not from the college town, not from Austin, Texas like himself, but he could not decipher what. An additional quick glance in her direction confirmed another rumbling thought gesticulating in the midlevel of his brain: he wanted to sleep with her.

—Let's blow this bitch. You want some soft-shell?

His buddy greeted him with a rowdy smile. Unfurling a hidden pack of maize tortilla from beneath his work shirt, he tossed the purloined package at Scott.

—I hope they fire your dumb ass, said Scott.

—Whatever, this job sucks.

—Man, at least jack something good, like maybe some chicken tortillas or chimichangas. Whata we supposed to do with these?

—Eat 'em, bitch, Scott's friend rejoined, laughing. He removed his mitered kitchen hat and dropped it into the passenger-side widow of the car. Grabbing back the plastic pack of circular bread from Scott, he ravaged a side of the bag to reveal the contents inside.

—Like this, Scott's friend said, ramming one full circle of corn tortilla inside his mouth.

Scott snatched the transparent package away from his thieving friend. He stuffed a single tortilla shell in his maw as well.

Inside the car, Scott tossed the flatbread onto the back seat. Before pulling out of the restaurant's parking lot, Scott stole a final look in the direction where the attractive woman had been waiting. She was gone.

Outside, evening had emerged, and with it a pleasant drop in the temperature. Neither Scott nor his friend felt any inclination to switch on the air conditioner.

—What'd Sarah say? Scott asked as he swiveled his boat onto the speedway that divided their university town in two.

—She can't come out tonight.

—Huh? Why not?

—She's gotta work.

—What work? She doesn't have a job.

—She got a job at Dreamers, just today actually.

—You mean the porn place? Scott laughed:

—That's awesome! So what's it like having a girlfriend working at an adult entertainment complex and, mind you, probably the best one in all of Austin, Texas!

His friend feigned a smirk:

—It's cool. We'll probably be able to get some free condoms or gels and stuff.

Scott's friend moved to turn on the radio.

Outside, the sun had disappeared, allowing the brisk hill-country breezes to spirit their zephyrs unhindered. A textbook, *US History: Reconstruction to World War II*, had rustled itself open from the youth's book bag. Scott suddenly realized his friend smelt vaguely of deep-fried fat and avocado. He rolled down all four windows. The untouched pages of the history book crinkled in the wind wildly.

Scott's expression became rueful:

—If your girl can't come out tonight, then who're we gonna get to buy us beers?

—I know somebody, his friend responded assuredly.

—Who?

—You know who.

Scott's mood soured:

—Damnit, you mean your suitemate, Thurston?

His friend answered in the affirmative.

—God, that guy is annoying.

—So? Who cares? He's not that bad anyway. Who else do we know that's not underage?

—I can't stand that cheesy Euro-trash thing he's got going on. Seriously, and his accent is retarded. It sounds like the way a computer talks or something.

—You just don't like him cuz he got with what's-her-name, the brunette chick you like in history class. But whatever, take this next exit. I already called him. He's waiting for us to pick up his sauerkraut ass.

In front of his friend's ancient-looking campus housing, Scott cursed when he saw that there were not any free slots to park his oversized car.

—Hurry up and call him, Scott ordered:

—I don't wanna have the car here like this, double-parked. Those campus police are dicks and are always out around here, giving out their stupid fake tickets and in those gay fake cop uniforms.

Scott's friend phoned his roommate, who appeared quickly thereafter, marching toward their car.

Thurston, the roommate, wore his t-shirt tucked tightly into his black-faded jeans. His sneakers, also black, were sparklingly new, so that the boy appeared tidier the lower one scanned his person. Speaking into his handset mobile, his voice was radiant, handsomely loud:

—Ja Ja! Ve vill be there at the party then soon. It is no problem, no problem, Thurston expounded into the phone.

He hung up and took his seat in the back of the Lincoln before greeting his ride.

—Vat's up, dudes?

Scott cringed at the resonating sound of Thurston's bellowing voice. His broadly continental accent grated at the driver's nerves. If Scott had traveled more, he would have recognized Thurston's timbre as being quite commendable, nominally clear—maybe even almost too concise at times—but never unintelligible. Unlike the majority of his northern European brethren back home along the borders of Germany and Switzerland, Thurston's dental fricatives, voiced or otherwise, were crisp and shapely defined: "thigh" and "thy" had never proved an obfuscation. His vowels were also well-rounded and beautifully pinpointed when need be, so that his voice conveyed an extra confidence that never ceased to charm any of the American co-eds within hearing distance. The only oddity that ever surfaced in the blond-headed boy's speech was an uncontrollable mixing-up of the Anglo "w" with a vibrating "v".

—Hey, Scott mumbled.

—Remember to bring your license? Thurston's roommate queried from shotgun.

—Ja, I have it.

Thurston pulled out his tawny, foreign-looking passport.

—Nah, I mean your driver's license. That ain't gonna work. Remember the last time? You got pissed off cuz the bouncers wouldn't let you go into any of the bars on Sixth Street. Same thing, man. You have to use your driver's license.

—This is shit. Vat is vrong vith this then, really?

Thurston brandished the front page of his passport. The lamination over his headshot, passport number, date of birth, and other essentials glistened colorfully in the sallow streetlight above.

—I know, I know. We've gone over this before. Just go get the new driver's license you got made when you came here to Texas so that we can buy some liquor.

—This is total shit, Thurston cursed, climbing out the Lincoln to head back indoors.

The street now sounded very quiet. Though there were many vehicles parked along the drive, the area in front of his friend's student housing seemed oddly barren.

Petulant, Scott grumbled:

—I really don't wanna hang out with this guy all night.

The boys waited for their beer-buying Aryan to descend again.

The emptiness of the street was finally rent by the taps of patent leather on old concrete. It was a sliding, rich-sounding tap that only ever comes from the soles of those who—romantically—eschew the newer marvels of plastic rubber for tanned leather.

Rotating his head toward the sound, Scott's friend commented on the lone walker rapidly approaching their car:

—Jigaboo at six o'clock.

—Huh?

—Nigger's coming.

Scott peered into his rearview mirror.

The looking glass displayed a tall man, well-proportioned, neither skinny nor large, like a runway model, moving towards the Lincoln along the sidewalk. His hair was cropped short and face clean-shaven.

Scott followed his progress toward them, noticing that the man's two-buttoned suit radiated wealth and that his tie was knotted high, not loosened in the least.

—Can you stop with the racist conservative shit already? Scott berated his friend.

—What? I didn't say nothing. Just pointing out that there was an Obama walking our way.

—Jesus, you can be retarded sometimes. Look, the guy's wearing like a suit and tie. He's probably a lawyer or something.

—Yeah, probably an ACLU lawyer going to waste tax-payer's dollars on some stupid affirmative action lawsuit or another, Scott's friend retorted.

As the man approached, they ceased their conversation and watched him stroll by. The back of his double-vented suit fluttered stylishly in the wind.

Scott gripped the steering wheel at ten and two tightly. Eyes still tracing the footsteps of the passing pedestrian,

Scott said to his friend:

—Fuck you.

He removed himself from the driver's seat and ran to catch up with the man.

Scott shouted to stop the stranger, who turned his head around. He stopped his stride.

—Hey...do you need like a ride or something? Scott asked, before awkwardly tagging a "sir" onto the end of the question.

The man studied the youth's face momentarily before responding:

—Are you student here?

—Uhh, yeah.

Starting to ambulate towards Scott, the man smiled.

—Yes, actually, I could use a ride. Or at the very least point me in the direction of the nearest gas station. I didn't seem to put enough gas in the rental and my phone battery is dead.

—Yeah, of course, Scott said, steering the stranger to his parked car:

—The gas station's kinda far, so you can't really walk. But I can give you a ride real quick. Are you not from 'round here?

—I've been invited to give a lecture. Do you know Professor Shaun? With the anthropology department? I'm here at his behest.

Scott answered in the negative. Any affirmative would have been a lie; he knew none of the names of his professors. He stopped the visiting professor in front of his vehicle.

—My Lincoln Continental, Scott expounded with gusto. He shouted to his friend to vacate the front passenger's seat:

—Out! We're giving the professor a ride.

—Oh, don't worry about it. It's all right. I can sit in the back, the man interrupted.

—No no no, see, he's already moving in the back. Take the front seat. Gas station's only like ten minutes anyway.

The professor circled the front hood and was going to take his seat when he saw the mess of not-completely-empty fast-food bags, plastic-coated paper cups, lids and indentured straws, a few crumbly piles of soiled napkins, all from dubious usage, and what looked like a college algebra textbook that was for some reason burnt on the edges.

Noticing the man's hesitation, Scott reached down to clean away as much of the filth that he could, tossing most of the refuse over the seat into the back, some of the mucky garbage hitting his friend's person.

With the majority of the trash gone, the professor unbuttoned his suit before sitting down.

Catching the mistrusting eyes of the driver's friend through the rearview mirror, the man extended his hand to the pair of students, introducing himself:

—Darrel Brown, professor of Anthropology, University of Michigan.

The boys greeted the man in kind, though both eschewed their surnames.

Ignition turned, the eight-cylinder engine started to rumble again warmly. Pulling away from the front of the student housing speedily, Scott saw the figure of the German youth exiting the building.

Thurston found himself bereft of transportation.

Scott smiled to himself.

Scott's friend kicked at the back of the driver's padded seat. He turned to see his comrade scrunching his face, mouthing the words: what about the beer?!?!

A cellular phone twinkled and vibrated from the back

seat, its ring tone a beepy rendition of some rap tune. Scott's friend answered. After minding the caller's conversation, he responded:

—All right, chill out already!

Scott's friend covered the mouthpiece:

—Looks like you pissed the German off. He wants us to go back and pick him up.

Shaking his head, Scott snorted.

It was time for Scott's friend to feel petulant. He yelled into the mobile:

—We're coming already. Just wait a sec! He then ended the call.

The professor broke in:

—I hope I'm not causing you two too much of a problem?

—Awh, no, don't worry about that. Look, there's the gas station right there. They probably have those plastic gas canisters that you can fill up with a gallon or two.

Scott stopped his vehicle as the swaying traffic light blinked from green to red.

Out on the city's main thoroughfare, the activity of young collegians ruckusing about and working folks journeying home for the evening was at a normal pitch. Everyone seemed to be blissfully ignoring everyone else. Stationary for the moment, a city bus emptied a score of individuals onto the adjacent sidewalk. The majority of commuters were clothed in various degrees of casualness: the younger the person, the more degenerate the casualness. All but a few of the commuters had stringy, gummy-like wires protruding from their ears to various orifices hidden either within folds in their garments or in their carryon knapsacks, briefcases, or over-sized purses. A few held their music players in hand, too afraid to leave them unattended in a trouser pocket or backpack flap. One perambulator, dressed in mismatching suit jacket and slacks, was hurrying in front of the others. Even from a hundred paces away, where Scott sat with his foot on the brake, the rushing pedestrian's attire appeared hopelessly tawdry. The shoddy mass-produced tailoring of the man's dreary duds reminded Scott of the person sitting next him—reminded him how much better the anthropologist's apparel was. The professor looked more like an industrialist than an anthropologist.

—What are you two majoring in? The professor spoke, thinning the silence inside the Lincoln.

Scott responded first:

—Well, not sure yet. Still undeclared.

—Yeah, uh, me too, the friend answered likewise.

—It's just as well. You needn't rush a decision like that. You'll find something that excites you intellectually soon enough. You two freshmen? Sophomores?

—Sophomores, they responded simultaneously.

A homeless man wended his way through the nascent traffic gathering in front of the stoplight. He was filmed in a potent metropolitan menagerie of city dirt, tarry dreck particles, concrete dust, and bits of black spilth. The man was soiled as only one can be who exhausts his homeless evenings and nights meting out an existence amidst the ravels of society.

From somewhere, somehow, the mangy man had gotten hold of a dozen or so puce roses. He waved them about to the uninterested persons inside each of the vehicles he passed. His gait had an extra limping bounce, as if he had survived a car accident. Each time he hobbled up to his next customer, he would smile, proffer a retarded jig, and end his seller's escapade with a dimwittedly charming countenance.

Scott watched him perform his hitherto unsuccessful

tourney of moneymaking for the sedan in front of them. The child in the sedan's backseat clapped his hands when the tramp began his dance. The adult operating the vehicle in the driver's seat shushed the five-year-old, ordering him to ignore the homeless errant outside.

Unsuccessful again, the man traveled onto the next car stuck in traffic. Still unsuccessful, the dusty vagabond moved toward the Lincoln, catching the eye of its driver.

Scott was unable to roll up the windows in enough time.

—Red, pussy-sweet roses! Red, pussy-sweet roses! The man sung in exalted turpitude.

He grinned playfully at the college students in the Lincoln:

—You boys know what these are?

Neither one of the students nor the professor answered.

—These are pussy-catchers! You take one, put it up to the female, and then the female gets catched. And then she gets all wet.

The vagrant cackled:

—That's why I call 'em pussy-catchers! But yah know what else I likes to call 'em? Pussy-sweet! Pussy-sweet, cuz they sweet—just like the pussy. How many you boys want? How 'bout this: one for each of yah.

The seller peered lower into the Lincoln until he spotted the professor.

—Say brother! Can yah help a fellow nigger out?

Refusing to reply, the anthropologist parried by locking his gaze to the horizon. He kept his face forward until the stoplight along W Martin Luther King Jr Blvd glowed green, allowing Scott to drive away from the libertine bum.

Scott's mobile jingled a few high-pitched beeps. Removing the folded device from his jeans, he unfurled the chrome-colored phone to read the incoming message, keeping his other hand upon the steering wheel. As he pulled into the gas station he read his friend's text:

—SURPRISED U DIDNT GIVE HIM A RIDE 2!!

Scott chucked his phone at his friend in the back, but he dodged the projectile easily.

With the car now parked in front of the petrol station, the anthropologist moved to exit the Lincoln.

—Ummm, professor, I was wondering if you could maybe help us buy some stuff. We're heading to a friend's house and we, like, need to get some beer. Do you think you could buy it for us real quick? Here's a twenty, Scott mumbled, handing the man a warm, wrinkled bill from his jeans pocket.

The professor stared down at the university student. A mischievous smile then broke across the elder's face, an amused countenance as winning as his threads.

—Well, that takes some gusto: asking one of your professors to procure liquor for you. If we were in Ann Arbor, I doubt that I'd grant you your request. But since we're so far away from that cold place and I'm feeling in an obliging mood tonight, I suppose I could be convinced to help out a couple of sordid sophomores like yourselves.

The professor chuckled.

—All right, but you have to do two things for me. First, you have to promise not to tell anyone I'm doing this. And second, you both have to promise to major in anthropology, the professor bargained with the nubile scholars, knowing full well that neither promises would survive unpolluted beyond the present evening.

The professor snatched away the twenty dollars after the students gave their word.

—What kind of beer do you kids drink around here

anyway? Lone Star, right? I recall seeing some movie set in Texas where everyone drank Lone Star Beer.

—Oh no, sir, that's okay. Actually just like some Bud or Bud Light. Nobody really drinks that Lone Star stuff. If we do drink a Texan beer, we normally just drink Shiner.

—Speak for yourself, piped up a disgruntled voice from the backseat:

—I think Lone Star's pretty good. Cheaper than Shiner or Budweiser, too!

—Bud Light's fine, Scott reiterated.

—Right. Bud Light then, the professor whistled laconically as he got out of the Lincoln.

As soon as the visiting professor had slipped into the mini-market that hung desperately onto the side of the gas pumps, much like it hung onto the oil industry as a whole, Scott's friend quipped:

—You're crazy, asking a teacher to buy us beer.

—Whatever. He's doing it, isn't he? Now we don't have to worry about the German.

—I'm not the one worried about him. You are cuz you think he's gonna hit on all the girls you wanna talk to, Scott's friend scoffed.

Thinking over the upcoming events scheduled for the night, Scott Ehrlich did not retort.

Scott also mulled over his companion's not-so-latent racialism, weighing the good he knew of him against this one particular perversion.

Having grown up with other children whose ethnic inheritance was as zestfully multifarious and colorfully piquant as a well-stocked spice cabinet, Scott wondered sometimes at his friend's comments. Scott had been brought up in Austin's suburbs. He knew that one could not survive through middle or high school saying such things; those older ideas sometimes mumbled by a grand-parent or disgruntled uncle would have led to a cudgeling on the schoolyard. One would not have been able to find any playmates to patter about with.

Worse still, Scott thought, a fear of dabbling in miscegenation would have meant severely limiting one's options for getting laid. Scott recounted the time his friend had bragged that he had only ever been with Caucasian girls. That his compatriot allowed bigotry to corrupt his game was bedlam. Not until college had Scott met people similar to his friend—people normally from the west of the state or from one of those dreary towns that littered the highway corridors connecting Dallas to Austin to San Antonio to Houston—who actually cultivated a worldview manacled to the shade of one's epidermis.

Scott's companion in the backseat spoke up again:

—Shit! I think I ate too many of those leftover refried beans. Wait for me a sec. I gotta drop the Cosby kids off at the pool!

Scott's friend dashed into the minimart, returning a moment later with a key dangling from a dirty piece of duct-taped plastic and wood. Someone had marked a large M-E-N onto the oversized keychain. Seeing the washroom on the other side of the building, the boy rounded the structure quickly and went in.

Bright red plaster canister in one hand, twenty-four pack of mass-marketed beer in the other: the professor emerged from the convenience store, walking toward the unmanned pump.

Scott left his vehicle to assist his beer-buying benefactor. After the two gallon tank had been leveled off with low-grade petrol, the man did not argue with the student when he offered to carry the two items back to the Lincoln. Scott, pleased to have the spirits in his possession now, placed both the gasoline container and the box of malted goods into his already overcrowded trunk. Pushing some rainswept camping gear aside, shoving some older textbooks to another corner, he was able to nestle the new items in snuggly. The professor was already seated in shotgun.

Once inside the front of the heavy automobile, Scott immediately started the Lincoln and pulled out onto the street.

—Where did your car run out of gas? Scott asked.

—I think it was just off MLK, up here a bit. At least I think it was MLK anyway. It seems every city I visit has a Martin Luther King Jr. Drive or Street or Road or Boulevard in it.

The professor thought to himself before adding:

—In fact, would one even want to live in an American town that did not have a street named MLK in it?

Scott agreed.

The professor's vision passed over the rearview mirror. He noticed for the first time that the driver's companion was not in the backseat.

—Where did your friend go?

The night air was now inundated with cool winds, gentle and wet, wafts of country atmosphere that only ever rolled into the college-town capitol after the sun's departure.

—He's not really my friend. He's kind of an asshole, actually.

The nineteen eighty-two Lincoln, as it passed by some knockabout youths walking toward one of the city's many fraternity houses, appeared even more mammoth-like under the yellowy streetlamps.

Rooftop

The Nigerian study-abroad student sat facing her laptop, somewhat hypnotized by the cursor's blinking metronome. Beginning an essay was always the most difficult step, she thought.

Outside her shared dorm room, down the hallway, a coed screamed playfully. Nkoyo turned away from the blank document toward the shut door. Maybe she would be able to concentrate better if she got away from the dormitory? But she knew that would only be an excuse; she was procrastinating. Another boisterous cry from somewhere in the corridor, however, finally convinced her otherwise.

Closing her notebook, she deposited the device and the three Chinua Achebe novels that her paper was supposed to critique into her Texas Tech backpack. Nkoyo entered the hallway and walked toward the lift.

The elevator carried her to the top floor where she exited. To get to the rooftop though, one had to forego the lift and walk the last flight of unadorned stairs. No students were allowed on the roof, but Nkoyo guessed no one would be out monitoring. No one would fret about a lonely female literature major salting herself away for the afternoon on an unused rooftop.

An autumn zephyr welcomed her immediately as she stepped out onto the barren rooftop of the twelve-story high structure. She unfurled the arms of her red hoodie to block the wind. Nkoyo quickly found her normal writing spot near the building's industrial-sized air ducts. Comfortable, she removed her books and laptop. Another gust of wind blew westerly, rustling the highlighted pages of the topmost stack of used books.

She picked up her copy of *Things Fall Apart* and thumbed through the pages listlessly, blankly until she came to last page with Achebe's black-and-white portrait.

Nkoyo sighed.

Admitting that she thought Achebe's prose not worth analyzing in depth had surprised her professor. The frail lecturer could not understand why Nkoyo would not want to write on this world-renown author of her own nation. Was there any better known African writer? the lecturer had questioned. But Nkoyo was used to such silent admonishments: when her father had carried their family to London to work with the oil giants, her college professors had also not understood why such a bright girl like Nkoyo could not seem to embrace such a cultural treasure. Surely all Nigerians loved Achebe. Not this one, she would think to herself. Nkoyo was going through a *fin-de-siècle* phase, where if the writer was not a realist and not dead by at least a century, then she was not interested. She would have taken a lesser work by de Maupassant, Galdós, or even Fontane over any of Achebe's supposed bests.

Now that her father had been relocated to Irving, Texas, she had followed the family again dutifully and ended up in some place called Lubbock for her masters' degree. Here, the water was not safe to drink, and the air smelt of burnt tires in the summer. Lagos had a similar smell, she would occasionally remind herself.

Nkoyo had attempted to be conciliatory to her new professor. If they insisted that she critique someone from her native continent, how about Tayeb Salih, or even better, Coetzee? she had suggested. Neither of those had esteemed her to Nkoyo's instructor: one was too Arabic, and as for Coetzee—did he even count, an Afrikaner?

Also, Nkoyo's ethnic group was Yoruba and Achebe's Igbo, but that actually mattered little to her, cosmopolitanized girl that she was, half raised in London, half in Lagos. She had even met Achebe once. Her father's wealth had allowed them to move through the type of social class that inevitably draws in national literati from time to time.

—Our daughter aspires to be a writer, Nkoyo's father had said after dragging her away from her peers.

The family was celebrating their last evening in Lagos before the big move to London. The city's socialites had gathered at their downtown loft. Achebe had been dragged along by one of these affected souls, unwillingly. But the bookish man was experienced enough to know not to fight his public role:

—A youthful woman author, strong and confident, that would surely mix up the old club of writers here in Nigeria, Achebe responded, shaking hands with the fifteen-year-old Nkoyo.

Achebe knew immediately when he was in the midst of an unforgiving critic. The precocious glint off Nkoyo's eyes told him so.

—And who is your favorite author then? Achebe continued.

Nkoyo did not answer immediately, so her father, standing behind her, squeezed her shoulder, indicating that she stop playing the boarding school brat and respond to this living national icon in front of her.

Deviously, Nkoyo smiled:

—I love Conrad.

Before Achebe could answer, Nkoyo wriggled away from her father and hid amongst her friends.

Nkoyo's father laughed magnanimously. The oil man had never heard of Conrad before.

—You have to forgive her. You understand how teenagers are. But she sure does think your writing's swell, Mr. Achebe. She was just telling me the other day she hopes to emulate your style, Nkoyo's father said to the Nigerian hero.

As Nkoyo was recounting these memories, still staring at an empty word processer document, she heard the sound of the stairwell's steel-hard door open and close quickly. From behind the air duct she could not see who had entered onto the roof.

A man appeared and walked indolently to the building's precipice. He did not espy the exchange student. With his back to Nkoyo, the man removed a cigarette from his uniform windbreaker.

Nkoyo recognized him as the complex's security guard. He was a Nigerian, an Igbo like Achebe, and had conversed with Nkoyo a few times, but only enough to establish that he was a poorer immigrant—probably with refugee status, she guessed—and that he was much too diffident for a Nigerian male.

—Ikenna! You can't smoke up here, Nkoyo shouted at his back coltishly.

The security guard appeared startled, as if someone had just ran a feather against the back of his neck, and immediately dropped his fugitive cigarette. Turning to face his accuser, Ikenna relaxed when he saw Nkoyo's friendly, smiling countenance. Embarrassingly, Ikenna walked towards his impish compatriot.

—Little sister, what are you doing on the roof here?

Ikenna smiled when he spoke. His eyes seemed to hold a thousand starry stories. All the men of Lagos seem to have eyes like this, she thought as he neared her—eyes

114

that were always shiny, both somehow religious and lecherous at the same time.

—I'm not your sister. And smoking is like a sin in America, so maybe they should fire you, she rejoined.

—Fire me? But fire me how? I am a star employee of the university. And if I have to go, then who would watch over you, little sister?

Ikenna's voice carried the weight of his forefathers. His accent was terribly Sub-Saharan, rusted by a not-so-distant colonization, limned with unforgiving experience, yet veneered, coated anew with something hopeful and forward-looking all the same.

Ikenna crouched down in front of the coed. If someone had walked upon the two, they may have thought the uniformed man was leaning over to kiss Nkoyo. Ikenna picked up one of her paperbacks.

—Uncle Chinua! He is like me; he is Igbo, Ikenna said when he saw the cover.

Nkoyo watched him turn the book over. She wondered why the way one cradles a book in is one's hands is always a giveaway; Nkoyo wondered if the security guard had ever read a novel.

Ikenna suddenly appeared tired:

—I cannot be a university student. You see me, little sister, how I am already old. So I cannot be a student. But I know this story.

—The writing's just okay, Nkoyo replied, a hint of honest London listlessness highlighting her accent.

Ikenna turned over the paperback again.

—This story is about my mother's mother's village. Or, no, maybe my grandmother's mother's village. But, it is about a village in the east of the country.

Ikenna placed the book atop the other two carefully.

—Little sister, do you miss Nigeria?

Another gust of wind blew, this time from the north. The wisps of cooler air flipped open and closed the cover of the topmost book.

Nkoyo did not respond. She did not want to answer Ikenna's question.

The security guard's radio beeped. Someone's voice crinkled through the walkie-talkie unintelligibly. Ikenna stood and retrieved the plastic-cased device from his belt. He spoke into the receiver once, quickly, before returning the radio to its holster.

Ikenna smiled down at Nkoyo.

—That is okay. I do not miss Nigeria anymore either, little sister.

The security guard hurried away, leaving Nkoyo alone on the roof. She closed her laptop, placing it aside, and walked to the edge of the roof. Once to the cement precipice, atop the twelve-story building, she peered over the edge into the afternoon horizon, her back to the wind, her dark-brown eyes forward, gazing upon the flat interminable plains of the Texas panhandle.

Nkoyo returned to her special writing nook and began her essay, not the one on Achebe, but the one she wanted to compose on de Maupassant.

About the Author

T. F. Rhoden's first eighteen years or so all belong to the Republic of Texas. Then, in the summer, Rhoden left, went to Western Europe, continued going East, before settling in Southeast Asia. The beer was better in Europe. Yet the tropics are lush.

Once Rhoden fell into a brackish pothole in downtown Yangon. Rhoden's favorite phrase in Czech was *Potřebuju tři piva, prosím*. The more attractive daughters of Indian oligarchs advise against eating street food. Rhoden has a BA, a MBA, and is now studying a PhD. You shall meet many a Russian in Dubai. Rhoden remembers donning green shoes for an assent of Tai Shan. Three days ago our dog had four puppies. The misses suggests we keep the whitest one.

None of us wishes to abandon stereotypes if we don't have to. Their utility is unquestionable. Yet, this anthology cares little about all of that. Occasionally, the sensation of sheepishness often associated with a change in one's understanding of a place or a time is well worth the trial in self-reflection. This is, of course, occasionally.

The Irish apostate James Joyce succeeded in secularizing the term "epiphany" for literature. The book in your hands now, entitled *Texaners*, borrows unabashedly from Joyce's insight. *Texaners* is, naturally, inspired by Joyce's *Dubliners*. Impish errors aside, why else bother really?

The less we broad upon experience the better. Time for a Thai massage.

Contact at www.tfrhoden.com.

Étoile

Solitaire
Press

www.ingramcontent.com/pod-product-compliance
Lightning Source LLC
Chambersburg PA
CBHW051110030726
47504CB00006B/1878